THE BOY WHO KNEW

WHAT

THE BIRDS SAID

The Boy Who Knew What The Birds Said

Padraic Colum

Illustrated by Dugald Stewart Walker

ISBN 13: 978-1475290738

ISBN10: 147529073X

***

Pied Piper Press

piedpiperpress@gmail.com

First edition: May 2012

Printed in the United States

THE BOY WHO KNEW WHAT THE BIRDS SAID

PADRAIC COLUM

ILLUSTRATED BY
DUGALD STEWART WALKER

CONTENTS

Introduction

Written over a hundred years ago this book still has a fresh and exciting voice. The tales that are told touch us deeply in our soul, awakening our imagination and spurring us to inner action. I hope you come to love it as much as I have.

I have edited it with a light hand, mostly to clarify when the story thread wandered off track, and to footnote words that are uncommon, are Celtic in origin, or which have fallen out of use. I also changed a couple of the Gaelic spellings—impossible to pronounce!—into related names friendlier to our comtemporary tongue.

I have included, at the back of the book, a section on the birds mentioned in the tales. Some because they are unknown in North America, but others because we have grown so citified that the average person no longer automatically knows many birds by sight and flight. If there is a bird you are unsure about, just go to the back and look it up.

Also mentioned in one tale is Ogham writing and so I have included a couple of pages on this interesting and unique alphabet for you to explore—and even write yourself.

Enjoy! ~ Reg Down

HOW HE CAME TO KNOW WHAT THE BIRDS SAID

THERE is one thing that all the birds are afraid of, and that is the thing that will happen when the Bird-That-Follows-The-Cuckoo flies into the cuckoo's mouth.

"And will happen then?" asks my kind foster-child and listener.

When the Bird-That-Follows-The-Cuckoo flies into the cuckoo's mouth the world will come to an end. All the birds know that, but not all the people know it.

Well, one day the cuckoo was sitting on a bush and her mouth was open. The Bird-That-Follows-The-Cuckoo flew straight at it—and into it he must have flown ... only for the Boy. The Boy was in the tree and he flung his cap at the cuckoo and it covered the cuckoo and the cuckoo's open mouth.

The Bird-That-Follows-The-Cuckoo flew into the crow's mouth instead, and the crow gave that bird a squeeze, I can tell you. The cuckoo pushed off the Boy's cap with her wings and flew into the forest.

All the birds of the King's garden were there at the time. There were:—

The crow, the woodpecker,
The wren and the eagle,
The blackbird and swallow,
The jackdaw and starling,
And the wonderful peacock;
The lapwing and peewit,
The bold yellowhammer,
The bad willy-wagtail,
The raven so awful,

And the cock with his hens;
stone-checker, hedge sparrow,
And lint-white and lark,
The tom-tit and linnet,
And brisk little sparrow,
The kingfisher too,
And my own little goldfinch.[1]

All the birds in the King's garden were overjoyed that the Bird-That-Follows-The-Cuckoo did not get into the cuckoo's mouth.

"What shall we do for the boy who prevented the world from coming to an end?" asked the good-natured corncrake.

She was there too, but I forgot to mention her.

"Nothing," said the willy-wagtail. "The boy who would throw a cap would throw a stone. Do nothing at all for him."

"I'll sing for him," said the goldfinch.

"I'll teach him what the birds say," said the crow.

"If he knew the language of the birds he would be like King Solomon," said the raven.

"Let us make him like King Solomon," said the goldfinch.

"Yes, yes, yes," said all the birds in the King's garden.

---

1) See pages 149-150 for descriptions and illustrations of all the birds mentioned in this book.

The Boy had not gone far when the crow flew after him and lighted on his shoulder. The crow spoke to him in the Boy's own language. The Boy was surprised. The crow flew to a standing stone[2] and went on speaking plain words to him.

"O," said the Boy, "I didn't know you could speak."

"Why shouldn't I know how to speak!" said the crow. "Haven't I, for a hundred years and more, been watching men and listening to their words? Why shouldn't I be able to speak?"

"And you can speak well, ma'am," said the Boy, not forgetting his manners.

"You know one language, but I know many languages," said the crow, "for I know what people say, and I know what all the birds say."

The old crow sat there looking so wise and so friendly that the Boy began to talk to her at his ease. And after a while the Boy said, "Ma'am, do you think I could ever learn what the birds say?"

"You would, if you had me to teach you," said the crow.

"And will you teach me, ma'am?" said the Boy.

"I will," said the crow.

---

2) Standing stones were erected thousands of years ago—about 3000-1500 BCE. They are often associated with the Druids, the priests of the ancient Celtic people.

Then every day after that the crow would sit upon the standing stone and the Boy would stand beside it. When the crow had eaten the boiled potato that the Boy always brought she would tell him about the languages of the different birds. The two were teaching and learning from day to day, and indeed you might say that the Boy went to school to the crow. He learnt the language of this bird and that bird, and as he learnt their languages, many's and many's the good story he heard them tell each other.

THE STONE OF VICTORY

THE STONE OF VICTORY

AND HOW FEET-IN-THE-ASHES, THE SWINEHERD'S SON, CAME TO FIND IT

"IF we went there, if we went there, maybe we'd find it," said the cock-grouse to the hen-grouse as they went together, clucking through the heather.

"And if we found it, if we found it, what good would the Stone of Victory do us?" said the hen-grouse to the cock-grouse, answering him back.

"And what good did the Stone of Victory do to the youth who was called Feet-in-the-Ashes, and who was only the swineherd's son?" said the cock-grouse to the hen-grouse.

"Tell me, tell me, and then I shall know," said the hen-grouse to the cock-grouse, answering him back.

They went together, clucking through the heather and the Boy-Who-Knew-What-The-Birds-Said followed them.

He lay upon a rock and the cock-grouse and the hen-grouse spoke below him, the cock-grouse always lifting his voice above the hen's. The Boy heard what they said and he remembered every word of it. And, by the tongue in my mouth, here is the story he heard:—

Cluck-ee, cluck-ee, cluck-ee, cloo, cloo, cloo—The King of Ireland stood outside the gate of his castle and his powerful captains and his strong-armed guards were all around him. And one his captains went to the mound before him and he gave a shout to the east and a shout to the west and a shout to the north and a shout to the south. When the King asked him why he did it the captain said, "I want the four quarters of the world to know that the King of Ireland stands here with his powerful captains and his strong armed guards that no one dare come from the east or west, the north or the south and lay the weight of a finger upon him."

And when he said this the other captains flashed their swords and the guards clashed their shields and the King of Ireland said, "Well and faithfully am

I guarded indeed, and luckier am I than any other King on the earth, for no one can come from the east or the west, the north or the south and lay the weight of their finger upon me."

But no sooner did he say that than they saw a giant coming across the hill towards the place where they were standing. And when the giant came to them he lifted up his hand and he doubled his hand into a fist and he struck the King of Ireland full in the mouth and knocked out three of his teeth. He picked the King's teeth up, put them in his pouch and without one word walked past them and went down to the sea.

"Who will avenge the insult put upon me?" asked the King of Ireland. "And which of my captains will go and win back for me the three best teeth I had?"

But not one of his captains made a step after the giant.

"I know now," said the King, "how well you serve and how well you guard me. Well, if none of you will help me and if none of you will avenge me, I'll find those who will. And now I'll make a proclamation and I'll solemnly declare that whoever avenges the insult offered to me, and, in addition, brings back to me the three that were the best teeth in my head, even though he be a servant or the son of a servant, I'll give him my daughter in marriage and a quarter of my kingdom. And, more than that," said he, "I'll make him full captain over all my guards."

The proclamation was sent all over the castle and in the end it came to the ears of the swineherd's son who was called Feet-in-the-Ashes. When he heard it he rubbed the ashes out of his hair and said to his grandmother: "If there is anything in the world I want it is the King's daughter in marriage and a quarter of the kingdom. I'll want provision for my journey," said he. "So, grandmother, bake a cake for me."

"I'll do better than that for you, honey, if you are going to win back the King's teeth and marry the King's daughter," said his grandmother. "I have a few things of my own that no one knows anything about, and I'll give them to you with your cake. Here," said she, "is my crutch. Follow the giant's tracks until you come to the sea, throw the crutch into the sea and it will become a boat, step into the boat and in it you can sail over to the Green Island that the giant rules. And here's this pot of balsam. No matter how deep or deadly the sword-cut or the spear-thrust wound is, if you rub this balsam over it, it will be cured. Here's your cake too. Leave good luck behind you and take good luck with you, and be off now on your journey."

"And why was the youth called Feet-in-the-Ashes?" said the hen-grouse to the cock-grouse.

"He was called Feet-in-the-Ashes," said the cock-grouse, "because he sat in the chimney corner from the time he could stand upon two legs. And everybody who called him Feet-in-the-Ashes thought he was too lazy to do anything else."

Well, he left good-luck behind him and he took good-luck with him and he started off on his journey with the cake, the crutch and the cure. He followed the giant's tracks until they came down to the sea. Into the sea he flung his grandmother's crutch. It became a boat with masts and sails. He jumped into the boat, and the things that had to be done in a boat were done by him—

He hoisted the sails—the red sail,
the black sail and the speckled sail,
He gave her prow to the sea
and her stern to the land,
The blue sea was flashing,
The green sea was lashing,
But on they went with a breeze
that he himself would have chosen,
And the little creatures of the sea
sat up on their tails to watch his going.

And so he went until he came near the Green Island where Shamble-Shanks the giant who had carried off the three teeth of the King of Ireland had his castle and his stronghold.

He fastened his boat where a boat should be fastened and he went though the island until he came to a broad brown castle. No one was about it and he went through it, gate, court and hall. He found a chamber where a fire burned on the hearth-stone. He went to the fire gladly. He looked around the chamber and he saw three beds. "There's room to rest myself here, at all events," said Feet-in-the-Ashes.

Night came on and he left the fire and got into a bed. He pulled one of the soft skins over him. Just as he was going to turn on his side to sleep three youths came into the chamber. Feet-in-the-Ashes sat up on the bed to look at them.

When they saw him they began to moan and groan, and when he looked them over he saw they were all covered with wounds—with spear-thrusts and with sword-cuts. The sight of him in the bed, more than their wounds, made them moan and groan, and when he asked them why this was so the first of the three youths said:—

"We came here, the three of us, to fight the giant Shamble-Shanks and to take from this island the Stone of Victory. We came to this castle yesterday and we made three beds in this chamber so that after the combat we might rest ourselves and be healed so that we might be able to fight the giant again tomorrow or the day after, for we know that we cannot win victory over him until many combats are fought. Now we come back from our first fight and we find you in one of the beds we had made. We are not able to put you out of it. One of us must stay out of bed and the one that stays out will die tonight. Then we shall be only two against the giant and he will kill us when we come to combat again."

And when the first one had said all this the three youths began to moan and groan again.

Feet-in-the-Ashes got out of bed. "You can have your rest, the three of you," said he. "And as for me, I can sit by the fire with my feet in the ashes as often as I did before."

The three youths got into the three beds and when they were in them Feet-in-the-Ashes took the pot of balsam that his grandmother had given him and rubbed some of it on each one of them. In a while their pain and their weariness left them and their wounds closed up. Then the three youths sat up in their beds and they told Feet-in-the-Ashes their story.

"Cluck-ee, cluck-ee, cluck-ce, cluck, cluck," said the hen-grouse, "and what was the story they told?"

"Cluck, cluck," said the cock-grouse, "wait until you hear, cluck, cluck."

Said the first of these youths:— "On this island there is a moor, and on that moor there is a stone, and that stone is not known from other stones, but it is the Stone of Victory. The giant Shamble-Shanks has not been able to find it himself, but he fights with all who come here to seek it. Today we went to the moor. As soon as we got there the giant came out of his high Grey Castle and fought with us. We fought and we fought, but he wounded us so sorely that we were like to die of our wounds. We came back to rest here. Thanks to your balsam we are cured of our wounds. We'll go to fight the giant tomorrow, and with the surprise he'll get at seeing us again so soon we may be able to overcome him."

"And along with his surprise, there's another thing that will help you," said Feet-in-the-Ashes, "and that is myself. I have to fight him too and I may as well fight Shamble-Shanks in company as alone."

"Your help will be welcome if you have not come here to win the Stone of Victory."

"Not for the Stone of Victory I have come, but to win back the three teeth that were knocked out of the King of Ireland's head and to avenge the insult that was offered to him."

"Then we'll be glad of your help, good comrade."

The three youths got out of their beds and they sat with Feet-in-the-Ashes round the fire and the four spent a third of the night in pleasant storytelling, and slumber nor weariness did come near them at all.

"Cluck, cluck, cluck," said the hen-grouse.

"Say no more," said the cock-grouse, "for now I'm coming to what's wonderful in my story:—"

The four youths were seated round the fire when a little man came into the chamber. He carried a harp in his hands. He bowed low to each of the four of them. "I am MacDruide, the giant's harper," he said, "and I have come to play music for you."

"Not one tune do we want to hear from you," said Feet-in-the-Ashes.

"Whether you want it or not, one you will hear," said the harper, "and that tune is the Slumber Tune. I shall play it for you now. And if the whole world was before me when I play it, and if every one in it had the pains of deep wounds, the playing on my harp would make each and every one of them fall into a slumber."

"That tune we must not hear," said the first of the three youths, "for if we fall into a slumber the giant will see to it that we shall never awaken."

MacDruide, the giant's harper, put his harp to his chest and began to play. Slumber came on the eyelids of the four who were at the fire. Three sprang up, but one stayed on his bench dead-sound-fast asleep, one yawned and fell down on the floor, one of the two that remained went towards the harper, but on his way he fell across a bed and he remained on it. Then, out of the four, only one, Feet-in-the-Ashes, was left awake.

The harper played on. Feet-in-the-Ashes put his fingers in his mouth and started to gnaw them. He gnawed the first two fingers down to their joints. But still his mouth kept open in a yawn and still the slumber lay heavy on his eyelids. He gnawed his third and his little finger. Then he put his right hand in his mouth and he bit at his thumb and he bit so sharply that his senses nearly all came back to him. With a kick he knocked the harp out of the harper's hands. He caught MacDruide then and turned him head below heels and left him hanging by his feet from a beam across the chamber. Then he went straight through the hall and out of the castle.

A wet breeze was blowing and whatever sleep was on his eye it blew away. He walked on with the dark clouds of the night going behind him and the bright light of the day growing before him. "I'll turn back," said he, "when I hear a cock crowing, and whatever I find beside me I'll take to remind myself of where I have been."

He found himself on a moor and he walked on until he was far upon it.

A cock crew.

"Time to turn back," said Feet-in-the-Ashes.

He looked round to see what he might bring with him and he saw on the ground a round stone.

"A round stone?" said the hen-grouse.

"Yes," said the cock-grouse, "a round black stone. He took it up, that round black stone, and he went back to the castle, hungry for his breakfast."

In the castle chamber the three youths were still slumbering, one on the bench, one on the floor and one in a bed, and MacDruide the Harper was still hanging by his feet from the beam across the chamber.

"Lift me down from this, good lad," said the giant's harper.

"I will," said Feet-in-the-Ashes, "when my three companions awaken."

"They won't awaken," said MacDruide the Harper.

"Then you can hang there," said Feet-in-the-Ashes.

"They won't awaken," said MacDruide, "until I cause them to awaken, and I shall cause them to awaken if you lift me down from this."

"Will you promise by your head," said Feet-in-the-Ashes.

"By my head I promise," said the giant's harper.

Then Feet-in-the-Ashes lifted the harper down from the rafters and set him upon his legs. MacDruide took up the harp and he pulled the strings backways. The notes he drew out were so piercing that first one and then another and then a third of the three youths wakened up. Then, when they were on their feet, MacDruide the giant's harper, slipped out of the house and went away. What happened to him after that no one knows.

"Cluck, cluck," said the hen-grouse, "and what did they do after that?"

"The next thing they had to do," said the cock-grouse, drawing himself up, "was to fight. Yes, my lady, to fight."

The hen-grouse drooped her head and said no more, and the Cock-grouse went on valiantly—

Swords they drew out—the three youths who were with Feet-in-the-Ashes. They sharpened these swords. They marched off towards the moor with the swords in their hands. Feet-in-the-Ashes had no sword. All he had in his hand was a holly stick.

When they came in sight of the giant's Grey Castle they saw him come rushing out of the gate. He was clad all in iron and he had a sword in one hand and a spear in the other. The four youths spread themselves out so that they might be able to close round the giant. But for all his bigness the giant was quick enough. He struck one of them with his spear and brought him down on his knees. He struck the other with his sword and brought him down on his side. He struck the other with his iron-covered hand and brought him down on his back. And all that was left now was Feet-in-the-Ashes with his holly stick.

What could a youth with a holly-stick in his hand do against a giant that had a spear and a sword in his hands and was besides that all covered with iron? Feet-in-the-Ashes turned and ran! He ran towards the Grey Castle and went round it. And when he was at the east side the giant was at the north, and when he was at the south the giant was at the east. Round and round the castle they went and the giant with his strength and his quickness was wearing out Feet-in-the-Ashes.

Feet-in-the-Ashes wanted something to fling at him. He took the stone out of his pocket—the round black stone. He held it in his hand. He made three circles in the air with it. He flung the stone. It struck the giant on the breast and his iron breastplate rang as the stone struck it. Down fell the giant.

Feet-in-the-Ashes ran off to where his companions lay. Many times he looked back but he did not see the giant following him. The three youth were lying in their wounds and in their pain. Feet-in-the Ashes took out his pot of balsam and rubbed them all over.

Their wounds healed. First one stood up and then the second stood up and then the third stood up and the three were whole and well.

"Where is the giant?" each of them asked.

"Lying where he fell," said Feet-in-the-Ashes.

"And who threw him down?" said the first of the youths.

"I threw him down with a cast of a stone," said Feet-in-the-Ashes.

"Let us go and see," said the second of the youths.

They went towards the west side of the Grey Castle like men following a bear who might turn on them. The giant was lying still.

"He is dead," said one.

"He is dead indeed," said another.

"He is dead forever," said a third.

"He is dead by the cast of my stone," said Feet-in-the-Ashes.

They went up to where the giant was and looked him over.

"There is the stone that overthrew him," said one of the youths, pointing, "—that round black stone. Where did you get it?"

"On the moor," said Feet-in-the-Ashes.

"On the moor," said the others looking at him.

"Yes," said Feet-in-the-Ashes "I picked it up this morning on the moor just as the cock crew."

One of the three youths took the round black stone in his hand. "I'll bring the stone with me," said he. "We'll go into the castle now and see what our finding there will be."

They went into the Grey Castle. The three youths told Feet-in-the-Ashes they would help him to find what he had come to seek—the three teeth out of the head of the King of Ireland. They searched and they searched all over the castle. At last one of them opened an iron cupboard and there on a shelf was a silver cup and in the cup were three teeth. Feet-in-the-Ashes knew they were what he had come for and he put the cup in his pocket.

They took provisions from the giant's store, put them on the table and began to eat. But first one and then another and then the third of the three youths made an excuse and left the table. Feet-in-the-Ashes went on with his breakfast.

Then he left the castle to look for the three youths that had been his companions. He did not find them. He went down to the seashore. He saw his boat and the sails were raised on it. In the boat were the three youths and they were making ready to put out to sea. Feet-in-the-Ashes shouted to them. Then one of the youths came to the side of the deck and spoke back to him.

"You found the Stone of Victory without knowing it," said he, "and you let us take it in our hands. Now we cannot give it back to you for our lives depend on our keeping it and bringing it away. And," said he, "we fear to stay on the island with you because you have such luck that you could take the stone from us. The boat we came in is gone. We take your boat, but we think you have good luck before you and that you will find a way of getting off the island. Remember—what you came for was not the Stone of Victory but the King's teeth, and we helped find them for you."

They had hoisted the sails, and now a wind came and the boat that was from his grandmother's crutch was blown out of the harbor and Feet-in-the-Ashes was left without any companion on the island.

"Cluck, cluck, cluck," said the hen-grouse, "he found the Stone of Victory, but what good were his findings to him when he didn't know what he had found and let it be taken from him?"

"But if he hadn't found it he couldn't have slain the giant and taken the cup out of the iron cupboard—that much good the Stone of Victory did him," said the cock-grouse.

"I'm sorry to think that that's all he got from the Stone of Victory," said the hen-grouse.

"Well, that's all he got from it, and be quiet now till I tell you the rest of the story," said the cock-grouse.

Feet-in-the-Ashes went into the courtyard of the Grey Castle and he found there a great eagle that was chained to a rock. The eagle came towards him as far as the chain would let him.

"Feed me," said the eagle.

"Will you carry me to Ireland's ground if I feed you?" said Feet-in-the-Ashes.

"If you feed me every time I open my mouth, I will," said the eagle.

"That I'll try to do, good eagle," said Feet-in-the-Ashes.

He went through courtyard and penfold but not a sheep nor a pig nor a bullock[1] could he find. It seemed as if he would not be able to find meat for the eagle after all. He went down to the seashore and he came upon a pool filled with thin bony fish called skates. He took a basket of these and put it on his back. He came back to the courtyard and unlocked the chain that held the eagle.

"Feed me," said the eagle, and he opened his mouth.

"Close your eyes and I'll fill you mouth," said Feet-in-the-Ashes.

---

1) Bullock: a castrated (gelded) bull; a steer.

The eagle closed his eyes. Feet-in-the-Ashes flung a score[2] of skates into his mouth.

"Hard meat, hard meat," said the eagle, but he gulped them down.

Feet-in-the-Ashes, carrying the basket of skates on his back, put himself between the wings of the eagle. The eagle flew up and over the Grey Castle and faced for the plain of the sea.

They travelled from the morning light until the full noontide. The eagle opened his mouth again. Feet-in-the-Ashes put nothing into it. The eagle finding nothing in his mouth dropped down to the sea.

"Close you eyes," said Feet-in-the-Ashes," and I'll fill your mouth."

The eagle closed his eyes and Feet-in-the-Ashes put another score of skates into his mouth.

The eagle gulped them all down. "Whenever I open my mouth you will have to feed me," he said.

Feet-in-the-Ashes did not like to hear this, for a score more of skates were all that was left.

The eagle rose up again and on and on he flew until the night was coming over the water. He opened his mouth again. Feet-in-the-Ashes put in five more skates. The eagle kept his mouth open and said, "Feed me."

There was nothing to be done then but to put in the rest of the skates. Feet-in-the-Ashes flung them all

---

2) A score = 20.

in, and the eagle rose up and flew and they travelled while there was darkness on the water, and when the sun rose again Feet-in-the-Ashes saw they were flying over the land of Ireland. The eagle opened his mouth. Feet-in-the-Ashes had nothing to put into it.

"Fly on, good eagle," said he, "and leave me down at the King's Castle."

"Feed me," said the eagle.

"I will give you what you never had before," said Feet-in-the-Ashes, "—a whole bullock—when we come to the King's Castle."

"Cows far off have long horns," said the eagle, mocking him, and with that he flung Feet-in-the-Ashes off his back.

Sore would his fall have been if it hadn't been on a soft bog. On the softest of soft bogs he fell. He made a hole in the ground, but no bone in his body was broken. He rose up covered with mud and started off for the King's castle.

"Cluck, cluck," said the hen-grouse, "and did he not go to see his grandmother at all?"

"If he did it's not in the story," said the cock-grouse. "That very day, as I would have you know, the King was standing outside the gate of his castle with his powerful captains and his strong-armed guards around him.

'A year it is to-day,' said the King, 'since the giant came and struck me in the mouth, knocking out and taking away three of my teeth, and since that day I have had neither health nor prosperity. And you know,' said he, 'that my daughter and a quarter of my Kingdom is to go to the one who will avenge the insult and bring back my three teeth.'

'Such and such a thing prevented me from going,' said one of his captains, 'but now that so and so is done, I can go and avenge the insult offered to you.'

'So and so kept me from going,' said another of the captains, 'but now that such and such a thing is done I can go tomorrow and bring you back your three teeth.'

'I am tired of hearing you all talk,' said the King, 'and it's my belief that my teeth will be lost and my daughter unwedded till the day of doom.'

It was then that Feet-in-the-Ashes appeared before them. "Good health to you, King," said he.

"Good health to you, good man," said the King. "And what, may I ask, have you come here for?"

Feet-in-the-Ashes was covered with the feathers of the eagle and the mud of the bog, and, as you may be sure, the King and the captains and the guards looked sourly at him.

"I have come first of all, King," said he, "to give you advice."

"And what is your advice?" asked the King.

"My advice to you is that you send away all these you have around you—your captains and your guards—and that you turn them into dog-boys or horse-boys or anything else in which they would give useful service, for as they are here, they can neither serve nor guard you."

"All that may be true," said the King, "but what right have you to say it?"

Feet-in-the-Ashes said nothing but he held the cup up to the King. The King saw the three teeth in it and he took them out and placed them in his mouth and the teeth went into their places and there they firmly stayed.

Then Feet-in-the-Ashes told how he had gone to the Green Island and how he had avenged the insult offered to the king and found the teeth. Then he demanded the King's daughter in marriage and a quarter of the Kingdom, and both were made over to him on the spot.

As for the powerful captains and the strong-armed guards, some of them were made horse-boys and some were made dog-boys and Feet-in-the-Ashes was made captain over all the new guards. When he came to rule a quarter of the Kingdom he was given a horse and made a duke and was called by a better name than Feet-in-the-Ashes. But what that name was I don't remember now.

"Cluck, cluck, cluck," said the hen-grouse, "and did he go to visit the grandmother at all?"

"If he did," said the cock-grouse, "that's another story, and if it was ever told I don't remember it. Pray go to the right, my lady, for I'm hungry for the sweet buds of the heather."

THE KING OF THE BIRDS

THE KING OF THE BIRDS

THE thirteen little wrens sat on the apple-yard wall in the King's garden and their mother was there to teach them to fly. I call them the little wrens, but really each one was as big as their mother. She had a tail, however, that was most cunningly cocked and they had no tails, and the consequence was that when they made their little flights they always went sideways. Moreover, their beaks were still yellow and wide and open and this is always a sign of the young bird.

"All I ask of you," said the mother, "is that when you go into the world you remember that you are the children of the King of the Birds."

"Now why does our mother call us the children of the King of the Birds?" said one little wren to the other. "I think we're really very small. And I think our mother is very small. And there's our father behind that ivy leaf and he's very small too."

"And wherever you go," said the mother, "be sure to conduct yourselves like the children of the King of the Birds."

"It's because we were reared in such a fine nest," said another little wren. "No other birds in the world have such fine nests as we. That's the reason we're called the children of the King of the Birds."

"Men call the wren the King of the Birds," said the father wren, as he flew into a tree, "and surely men ought to know who is the King of the Birds."

"Why do men call the wren the King of the Birds?" asked the little wrens.

"I will tell you," said the mother. "As we fly from the wall to the tree, and from the tree back to the wall, I will tell you why men honor the wren as the King of the Birds," and she spent a whole day telling the little wrens the story and the Boy-Who-Knew-What-the-Birds-Said was there, and he heard the whole of it:—

The King of the Hither-side-of-the-Mountain conquered the two villages of Half-a-Loaf and Windy Gap, and the very day he conquered them he ordered the two headmen to come before him.

"You two headmen are to see that your villages, Half-a-Loaf and Windy Gap, send me my rightful tribute," said the King to them.

"There isn't much we can send," said the headman of Half-a-Loaf.

"A string of salmon," said the headman of Windy Gap.

"A basket of plover's eggs," said the headman of Half-a-Loaf.

"No," said the King, "the tribute that each of your villages must send me is the King of the Birds."

The two headmen went back to their villages, and that very day each told at the council what tribute the King had ordered them to send.

"The King of the Birds," said the people of Half-a-Loaf, "that's the eagle surely."

"The King of the Birds," said the people of Windy Gap, "what bird might that be? We'll have to give thought to this."

The people of Windy Gap thought about it and thought about it, but the people of Half-a-Loaf declared there was no doubt at all about it—the eagle was the King of the Birds. And while the people of Windy Gap were thinking and pondering, the people of Half-a-Loaf were sending their young men off to catch an eagle.

But an eagle is a hard fowl to catch, and the people of Half-a-Loaf found they had to send all of their young men out and to send them out every day. And the young men climbed high hills and stony ditches, and they searched the east and they hunted the west; they went out at sunrise and they came back at sunset, but never an eagle did they bring with them.

"It may be that the eagle is the King of the Birds," said the people of Windy Gap, "but we had better consider it."

They thought about it from sunrise to sunset; they thought about it while they plowed their fields and sowed them, while they spun their cloth and made their coats, while they mended their nets and mended their shoes, while they thatched their roofs and planted their apple-trees.

But in Half-a-Loaf there were few left to plow the fields and sow them, to spin cloth and to make coats, to mend nets and to mend shoes, to thatch roofs and to plant apple trees—there were few left to do these things, for all the young men were out on the mountain hunting for an eagle.

"The people of Windy Gap will be ruined," said the people of Half-a-Loaf. "They have done nothing yet to catch the eagle. When the King gets no tribute from them he'll sell them and their whole village. Call the young men back that have gone into the fields to work and send them up the mountain again."

At last the people of Half-a-Loaf caught their eagle—a great golden eagle he was. They built for him a shed and they fed him on what lambs they had that year.

"We're safe anyway," said the people of Half a-Loaf, "but the unfortunate folk in Windy Gap have lost their chance. They'll not have time to catch an eagle now."

The time was coming near when the two villages would have to send their tribute to the King.

"We have our eagle," said the people of Half-a-Loaf, "but O, bad fortune, we have hardly a crop growing! This will be a hard year for us—we haven't lambs to grow into sheep even."

"We have our crops," said the people of Windy-Gap, "but, bad cess to it! What are we to do about paying our tribute to the King?"

And still they couldn't decide whether it was the eagle or the cuckoo or the woodpecker that was King of the Birds. They were still considering it when the King's messenger came to bid them come with their tribute to the King's castle.

What were the people of Windy Gap to do? They searched round and about but no bird at all could they find. And then as he was being marched off the headman put his hand under the thatch of his house and took out a wren that was sheltering there. He put the wren under his hat and went off with the King's messenger.

And there, before him on the way to the castle was the headman of Half-a-Loaf. Riders of the village were with him and they bore their golden eagle most triumphantly.

"Give to my falconer the King of the Birds," said the King to the headmen.

The headman of Half-a-Loaf presented the eagle.

"It is well," said the King. "And what bird," said he to the headman of Windy Gap, "have you chosen as King of the Birds?"

The headman put his hand under his hat and handed over the wren to the King's falconer.

"Tush!" said the King. "Why do you call this the King of the Birds?"

The headman of Windy Gap was going to say, "Because his family is great," but he said instead, "Because he flies the highest, my lord."

"If it be the truth it's unknown to me," said the King, "but it shall be tried out."

Then said he to the royal falconer, "Let the eagle and the wren soar together—and when the eagle out-soars the wren it shall be proved that the headman of Windy Gap is a catiff,[1] and his village and everyone in it will be sold to the Saracens.[2] But if it so happens that the wren out-soars the eagle, the tribute sent from the village of Windy Gap must be accepted."

The eagle and the wren rose from the same perch and soared up together. Up and up the eagle went. "So far my father went, but I shall go farther," said the eagle. Higher and higher he rose. "So far my grandfather went but I shall go farther." Farther and farther he soared until his wings were stiff and tired. "So far my great-grandfather went and no eagle again will fly so high," said the eagle. "No bird will ever out-soar this flight of mine!"

He began to close his wings so that he might rest them as he went down—but as he did so the wren came out from under his feathers.

Up went the wren, down went the eagle. Up and up went the wren. He had been resting while

1) A contemptible or cowardly person.
2) A nomadic people of the deserts in the Middle East, between Syria and Arabia.

the eagle had been flying, and now he was able to soar past the point the eagle had reached at his dead-best.

The eagle flew down and lighted on the falconer's perch.

"Has he flown high, falconer?" asked the King.

"No bird has flown so high," said the falconer. "By the rime[3] on his wings he has gone into the line of frost."

"The eagle is King of the Birds and no one can deny it," said the King. "The village of Windy Gap has not sent me my tribute."

"Mercy," said the headman of Windy Gap.

"The village and all in it shall be sold to the Saracens," said the King.

Just then the wren came down and lighted on the perch beside the eagle.

"Where did the wren fly to?" asked the King.

"By my glove," said the falconer "he soared past the line of frost, and went into the line of snow, for what's on his feathers is a drop of snow."

"The wren is King of the Birds," said the headman of Windy Gap.

"Yes," said the King, "he is the King of the Birds and my lawful tribute!"

And so, for ever after the villages sent to the King, not an eagle, but a wren as tribute. And in no village

3) Rime: ice, frost.

ever after were the lands unplowed and the fields unsown, the cloth unspun and the coats not made, the roofs unthatched and the apple trees unplanted. And in every village in the hollow and on the height, the people shouted for the wren—"The wren, the wren, the King of all Birds."

BLOOM-OF-YOUTH
AND THE
WITCH-OF-THE-ELDERS

BLOOM-OF-YOUTH AND THE WITCH-OF-THE-ELDERS

Bloom-of-Youth was a young, young girl. But, young as she was, she would have to be married her stepmother said. Then married she was while she was still little enough to walk through the doorway of her stepmother's hut without stooping her head.

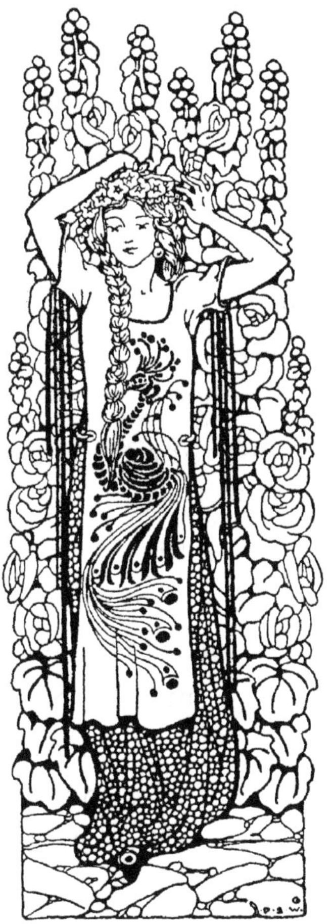

Her husband was a hunter and he took her to live in a hut at the edge of a wood. He was out hunting the whole of the day. Now what did Bloom-of-Youth do while she had the house to herself? Little enough, indeed. She swept the floor and she washed the dishes and she laid them back on their shelf. Then she went to the well for pails of water.

When she went out she stayed long, for first she would look into the well at her own image and then she would make a wreath of flowers and put it on her head and look at herself again. After that, maybe, she would delay to pick berries and eat them. Then she would go without hurrying along the path, singing to herself:—

"Said when he saw
Me all in blue,
'Who is the maid
The sky must woo?'

Said when he saw
Me all in green,
'Who is the maid
The grass calls queen?'"

When she got back to the hut the fire on the hearth would have gone out and she would have to light it again and then sweep the floor clear of the ashes that had blown upon it. After that she had little time to do anything else except prepare a meal against the time when her husband came back from hunting.

One morning her husband left his coat down on the bench. "My coat is torn; sew it for me," he said. Bloom-of-Youth said she would do that. But she did no more to the coat than take it up and leave it down again on the bench.

The next day her husband said, "My vest is torn too; have it and the coat sewn for me." He left the vest beside the coat and went out to his hunting.

Bloom-of-Youth did nothing to the coat and nothing to the vest, and every day for a week her husband went out without coat or vest upon him.

One day he put on his torn coat and his torn vest and went out to his hunting. When he came home that evening he had a bundle of wool with him.

Your stepmother sends you this bundle of wool," said he, "and she bids you spin it that there may be cloth for new clothes for me."

"I will spin it," said Bloom-of-Youth.

But the next day when her husband went away she did what she had always done before. She went to the well and looked for a long time at her image; she put a wreath of flowers on her head and she looked at her image again; she picked berries and ate them; she went along the path without hurrying, singing to herself:—

"Said when he saw
Me all in blue
'Who is the maid
The sky must woo?'

Said when he saw
Me all in green
'Who is the maid
The grass calls queen?'"

She had to light the fire again when she came in and sweep away the ashes that had gathered on the floor, and after she had done all that it was time to prepare the meal for the evening. But before her husband came home she took the spinning wheel out of the corner and put it near the light of the doorway.

"I see," said her husband, "that you are going to spin the wool for my clothes."

"I am when tomorrow comes," said Bloom-of-Youth.

But the next day she did as she done every day and no wool was spun. The day after that she put wool on the wheel and gave it a few turns. In a week from that evening she had one ball of thread spun.

"Your stepmother bids me ask you how much of the wool have you spun?" said her husband to her one evening.

Bloom-of-Youth was so much afraid that her husband would send her to her stepmother through the dark, dark wood, that she said, "I have spun many balls."

"Your stepmother bade me count the balls you have spun," said her husband.

"I will go up to the loft and throw them down to you and then you will throw them back to me and we will count them that way," said Bloom-of-Youth.

She went up to the loft and she flung down the ball she had spun.

"One," said her husband, and he threw it back to her.

She flung him the ball again.

"Two," said her husband, and he flung it back to her. Then he said "three," and then "four," and then "five," and so on until he had counted twelve. "You have done well," said he, "and now before the week is out take the twelve balls to your stepmother's house and she will weave the thread into cloth for clothes for me."

Bloom-of-Youth was greatly frightened. To her stepmother's house she would have to go with a dozen balls of thread in a few days. The next day she hurried back from the well and she sat at her wheel before the door spinning and spinning. But, do her best, she could not get a good thread spun in the long length of the day.

And while she was spinning and spinning and getting her thread knotted and broken, a hunched and crooked woman came and stood before the door.

"You're spinning hard I see," said she to Bloom-of-Youth.

Bloom-of-Youth gave her no answer but put her head against the wheel and cried and cried.

"And what would you say," said the old and crooked woman, "if I took the bundle of wool from you now and brought it back to you tomorrow spun into a dozen balls of thread?"

"It is not what I would say; it is what I should give you," said Bloom-of-Youth.

"Give me!" said the stooped and crooked woman. "What could you give me?" But as she said it she gave Bloom-of-Youth a baleful look[1] from under her leafy eyebrows. "No, no, you need give me nothing for spinning the wool for you. All that I'll ask is that you tell me my name within a week from this day."

"It will be easy to find out her name within a week," said Bloom-of-Youth to herself. She took the bundle of wool out of the basket and gave it to her.

1) A deadly, foreboding or evil look.

The craggy and crooked woman put the wool under her arm and then she lifted up her stick and shook it at Bloom-of-Youth. "And if you don't find out my name within a week you will have to give me your heart's blood—a drop of heart's blood for every ball of wool I spin for you."

The hag went away then and Bloom-of-Youth was greatly frightened, but after a while she said to herself, "I need not be afraid, for in a week I'll surely find out the name of the wizened and crooked woman who can't live far from this house."

The next day the hag came to the door and left twelve balls of wool on the bench outside the house. "In a week, in a week," said she, "you'll have my name or I'll have twelve drops of your heart's blood to make the leaves of my elder tree fresh and fine."

Bloom-of-Youth went with the twelve balls of wool to her stepmother's house, and every person she met on the way she asked if he or she knew the name of the crumpled and crooked woman—but no one could tell her the hag's real name. All they could tell was that she was the Witch-of-the-Elders and that she lived beside the Big Stones[2] that were at the other side of the wood.

Bloom-of-Youth was afraid: her face lost its color and her eyes grew wide and her heart beat from one side of her body to the other.

---

2) An ancient stone circle.

Every day the Witch-of-the-Elders would come to her door and say, "Have you my name yet, Bloom-of-Youth? Have you my name yet? Two days gone, five to come on; three days gone, four to come on; four days gone, three to come on; five days gone, two to come on."

Six days went by and on the seventh she would have to go to the Big Stones at the other side of the wood and let the Witch-of-the-Elders take twelve drops of her heart's blood.

The night before the week's end her husband, when he sat down by the fire, said, "I saw something and I heard something very strange when I was at the other side of the wood this evening."

"What was it you saw?" asked Bloom-of-Youth.

"Lights were all round the ring of Big Stones and there was a noise of spinning inside. That's what I saw."

"And what was it you heard?" asked Bloom-of-Youth.

"Someone singing to the wheel's turning," said her husband. "And this is what I heard sung:—

"Spin, wheel, spin; sing, wheel, sing;
Every stone in my yard, spin, spin, spin;
The thread is hers, the wool is mine;
Twelve drops from her heart will make my leaves shine!
How little she knows, the foolish thing,

That my name is Bolg and Curr and Carr,
That my name is Lurr and Lappie."

"O sing that song again," said Bloom-of-Youth. "Sing that song again."

Her husband sang it again, and Bloom-of-Youth went to bed, singing to herself:—

"My name is Bolg and Curr and Carr,
My name is Lurr and Lappie."

The next day, as soon as her husband had gone to his hunting, Bloom-of-Youth went though the wood towards the Big Stones that were at the other side of it. And as she went through the wood she sang:—

"Spin, wheel, spin; sing, wheel, sing;
Every branch on the tree, spin, spin, spin;
The wool is hers, the thread is fine;
For loss of my heart's blood I'll never dwine;[3]
Her name is Bolg and Curr and Carr,
Her name is Lurr and Lappie."

She went singing until she was through the wood and near the Big Stones. She went within their circle, and there, beside a flat stone that was on the ground, she saw the shriveled and crooked old woman.

3) Dwine: to waste away, to pine, to languish. Related to 'dwindle'.

"You have come to me, Bloom-of-Youth," said she. "Do you see the hollow that is in this stone? It is into this hollow that the drops of your heart's blood will have to run."

"The drops of my heart's blood may remain my own," said Bloom-of-Youth.

"No, no, they won't remain your own any longer when it is plain you can't tell me my name."

"Is it Bolg?" said Bloom-of Youth.

"Bolg is one of my names," screamed the Witch-of-the-Elders, "but one of my names won't let you go free."

"Is it Curr?"

"Curr is another of my names, but two names won't let you go free."

"Is it Carr?"

"Carr is another of my names, but three names will not let you go free."

"I know your other names too," said Bloom-of-Youth.

"Say them! Say them!" screamed the Witch-of-the-Elders.

But when she tried to think of them Bloom-of-Youth found that the last two names had gone out of her mind. Not for all the drops that were in her heart could she remember them.

"No, no, you can't say them," said the Witch-of-the-Elders. "And now bend your breast over the

D·S·W

hollow in the stone. I'll let out twelve drops of your heart's blood with my pointed rod. Bend your breast over the hollow."

But just as the witch was dragging her to the stone a robin began to sing on a branch outside the stone circle. It sang the same tune that Bloom-of-Youth had sung as she went through the wood. Now all the words in the song came back to her:—

"Spin, wheel, spin; sing, wheel, sing;
Every branch on the tree, spin, spin, spin;
The wool is hers, the thread is mine;
For loss of my heart's blood I'll never dwine!
Her name is Bolg and Curr and Carr,
Her name is Lurr and Lappie."

She said the last two names and as she did the Witch-of-the-Elders screamed and ran behind the stones and Bloom-of-Youth saw no more of her.

That evening her husband brought home the web of cloth that her stepmother had woven. The next day Bloom-of-Youth began to make clothes for him out of it. Never again did she make delays at the well but came straight home with her pails of water. The fire was always clear upon the hearth and she had never to light it the second time and sweep away the ashes that had gathered on the floor. She made good clothes for her husband out of the web of cloth her stepmother had woven. And every evening she spun on her wheel and there was never a time afterwards when she had not a dozen balls of thread in the house.

The wool is hers and the thread is mine;
For loss of my heart's blood I never will dwine,
And I throw my ball over to you.

It was the woodpecker that told this story to the Boy-Who-Knew-What-The-Birds-Said.

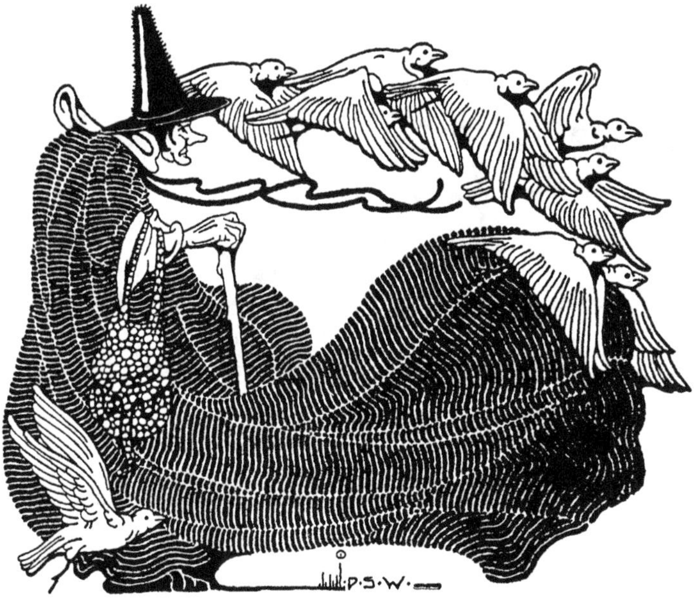

THE HEN-WIFE'S SON & THE PRINCESS BRIGHT BROW

THE HEN-WIFE'S SON & THE PRINCESS BRIGHT BROW

EVERYONE in and around the King's castle despised Mell, the hen-wife's son, said the stonechecker, the bird that built within the stones of the tower. And it was not because there was anything mean about the lad himself— it was because his mother, the hen-wife, had the lowest office about the King's castle.

This is what a hen-wife did: she had to mind the fowl and keep count of them, she had to gather the eggs and put them into a basket and send them to the King's steward every day. And for doing this she had as wages the right to go to the backdoor of the steward's house and get from the under-servants two meals a day for herself and Mell, her son.

And everybody, as I said, despised this son of hers—horse-boys and dog-boys and the grooms around the castle. But of course no one despised Mell more than did the King's daughter, Princess Bright Brow.

She used to go into a wood and whisper along the branch of a tree. And one day the hen-wife's son whom she despised so much made answer to her. He was lying along the branch of the tree, watching his mother's goat that grazed on the grass below. Now this is what Princess Bright Brow said to the tree, and this is what she used to say to it every day:—

"Oak-tree, oak-tree, above the rest,
Which of the heroes loves me best?"

Mell was lying along the branch as I have said, and he made answer back to her—

"Princess, Princess, he's at your call,
And the hen-wife's son loves you best of all!"

The King's daughter looked up and she saw the hen-wife's son on the branch, and she went into a great rage. She gave orders to the grooms that the hen-wife's son was to be whipped every time he looked at her. Many's the time after that Mell got the lash. But he loved Bright Brow so much that he could not forbear looking at her.

Now, one very early morning Mell took his mother's goat out to graze on the green beside a rath.[1] And as he went along he saw on the grass a beautiful mantle.[2] He took it up and he thought to himself, "How well it would look upon Princess Bright Brow!" And he thought again, "If she would take this beautiful green mantle from me maybe she would let me look upon her when she is wearing it."

He put the mantle across his shoulders and sat down and thought and thought. And while he was thinking he felt the mantle being pulled from behind. He turned round and he saw a woman standing there. She had brighter colors in her dress and wore more ornaments than anyone he had ever seen in the King's castle. He knew by such signs that she was a fairy woman out of the green rath.

"Mell," said she, "Mell, the hen-wife's son, give to me the mantle that the King of the Fairy Riders let fall from his shoulders last night."

---

1) Rath: earthen duns, or raths, are found all over Ireland. They were forts made of piled up earth. All that's left now are steep mounds with a flat top where the wooden walls and houses used to be. The fairies are said to live in them.

2) Mantle: a loose, sleeveless garment worn over other clothes; a cloak.

"If it is his, and if you have come to bring it to him, why you must have it," said Mell, and he took the mantle off his shoulders and handed it to her.

"The King would wish that I recompense you," said the fairy woman. She took a jewel that was on the collar of the mantle and gave it to Mell. "If you take this jewel in your hand," said she, "and wish to be in this place or that place you will be there in an instant, and anyone you take by the hand you can bring with you."

And when Mell took the jewel from her, the fairy woman, carrying the green mantle, went into the green rath.

Then Mell took his goat by the horns and turned towards his hut. And there, outside the gate of the castle, he saw the King's daughter, Princess Bright Brow. She was watching the falconer training the young hawks and the grooms and the riders of the castle were behind her. When she saw Mell with his hands on the goat's horns she grew high in rage and she turned to the grooms to give an order that he be beaten with the whips they held.

But Mell ran to her and he caught her hand and holding the jewel he said, "I wish that I was in the Island of the Shadow of the Stars and that this young girl was with me."

The hawk flew at him and the hound sprang at him and the whips struck at him and while he was still expecting to feel the teeth and claws and lash he was away and in another country altogether. There was neither hawk nor hound nor hut nor castle nor groom nor falconer. Two beings only were there and they were Mell, the hen-wife's son, and the King's daughter, Princess Bright Brow.

"In what country are we?" said Princess Bright Brow.

"Unless we are in the Island of the Shadow of the Stars I don't know where we are," said Mell, the hen-wife's son.

"You have brought me here by enchantment!" said Bright Brow in anger. She wanted to go from him, but where was she to go to? All the country was strange to her. And so, if she made two steps away from him she soon made two steps back to him. And the end of this part of the story is that Bright Brow became friendly to the hen-wife's son.

He gathered fruits off trees and he snared birds and he took the fish out of rivers and he found sheltered places to sleep in. And often Princess Bright Brow was good and kind to him. And Mell, the hen-wife's son, was now as happy as anyone in the world.

"Since we are so friendly to each other now," said Bright Brow to him one day, "will you not tell me how you were able to come here and bring me with you?"

"It was because of the jewel I wear at my breast," said Mell, and he told how he had found the green mantle on the ground and how the fairy woman gave him the jewel and what power the jewel had.

If Mell was content to be on the island, Bright Brow was not. And so one evening when he was asleep she took the jewel that was on his breast. Then holding it in her hand she said, "I wish I was back in my father's castle."

In an instant she was back there. Now all her maids were around her and all of them were crying,

"Where have you been, King's daughter, where have you been?" And Bright Brow told them that the King of the Fairy Riders had taken her away to show her all the great heroes of the world so that when the time came for her to choose a husband she could make her choice of the best amongst them.

As for Mell, the hen-wife's son, when he wakened and found that Bright Brow had gone, and that the jewel was gone, there was no one in the world more sad and lonely than he was. He thought that she might come back to him, but the moon came and the sun came and Bright Brow came not. He longed to be a bird that he might fly after her to her father's castle.

He stayed on the Island of the Shadow of the Stars for a long time, for now that the jewel was gone there was no way of getting from the island.

Then a King who had built a high tower went to the top of it one day and saw the Island of the Shadow of the Stars. He sent out his long ships and his leather-jerkined[3] men to it. They found Mell and they brought him to the King. Then Mell became one of the King's men and he went into battle and he learned the use of all arms.

Mell, the hen-wife's son, went through the Eastern and the Western Worlds and at last came

---

3) Jerkin: a close-fitting, hip length, usually sleeveless jacket.

back to where his mother's hut was. He rode round the walls of the King's castle. Everything that he thought was magnificent before seemed small to him now. The trees that grew within the walls seemed not much bigger than the bushes the old women put clothes to dry on.

Sitting on his black horse he looked across the wall that he once thought was so high and he saw the hen-wife's hut. His mother came out to feed the hens and to count them and to gather up the eggs and put them in a basket. "She's alive and I'll see her again," said Mell.

He rode round the wall to the King's garden to try to get sight the Princess Bright Brow. He saw no sign of her. He rode on and came to the gate at the other side and saw outside the cookhouse the horse-boys and dog-boys and grooms that he used to know. He saw them and he knew them, but they did not know him. He was surprised to see that they had not learnt to straighten up their shoulders, nor to walk as if there was a fine thought in their heads. They were all around the cookhouse and a great noise of rattling was coming from within it.

"What noise is that in the cookhouse?" Mell asked a groom.

"The cook's son is going out to fight," said the groom, "and he is striking the pot-lids with the ladles to let everyone in the cookhouse know how fierce he is."

"And who is the cook's son going to fight?" asked Mell, the hen-wife's son.

"He is going to fight a great champion that has come up from the sea in a boat that moves by itself. This champion demands that the King pay tribute to him, and the King has offered his daughter and half his kingdom to the youth who will go down to the seashore and defeat this champion. Today the cook's son is going out to make trial."

And while the groom was saying all this the cook's son came out of the cookhouse. His big face was all gray. His knees were knocking each other. The breastplate of iron he had on was slipping to one side and the big sword he had put in his belt was trailing on the ground.

"I would like to see what sort of a fight this champion will make," said Mell to himself. He followed the cook's son to the seashore—but the cook's son, when he had come to the shore, looked round and found a little cave in the face of the rock and climbed into it.

Then a boat that moved of itself came in from the sea, and a champion all in red sprang out of it. And when he had touched the shingles he struck his sword on his shield and shouted, "If the King of this land has a champion equal to the fray let him come forth against me. And if the King of the land has no such champion, let him pay me tribute from his kingdom."

Mell looked to the cave where the cook's son had hidden himself and all he saw there was a bush being pulled towards the opening to hide it.

Then Mell, the hen-wife's son, drew his sword and went down the beach towards the Red Champion.

They fought for half the day. At the end of that time the Red Champion said, "Good is the champion that the King of this land has sent against me. I did not know he had such a fine warrior."

They fought all over the strand, making the places that were stony, wet, and the places that were wet, stony, and then, when the sun was going down, the Red Champion was not able to do anything more than guard himself from the strokes of Mell's sword while he drew back towards his boat.

"You will have the honors of the fight to-day," said he to Mell.

"I shall have the honors and something else beside," said Mell. Then he struck at the red plume that was on his enemy's cap. He cut it off as the Red Champion sprang into the boat that moved of itself. As the sun was sinking the champion in the boat went away over the sea.

Now the cook's son had been watching the whole fight from the cave. When he saw the Red Champion going off in his boat he came running down to the shore. The hen-wife's son was lying with his hands and his face in the water to cool himself after the

·D·J·W·©

combat and the red plume that he had struck off the champion's cap was lying near him. The cook's son took up the plume.

"Let me keep this as a remembrance of your fight, brave warrior," said he to the hen-wife's son.

"You may keep it," said Mell.

Then with the red plume in his hands the cook's son ran back towards the castle.

Mell put on his best garments and went to the castle that evening and he was received by the King as a champion from foreign parts. And the King invited him to supper for three nights.

Princess Bright Brow was at the supper and Mell watched and watched her. He saw that she was pale and that she kept sighing. Of the damsel who sat beside him at the table Mell asked, "Why is the King's daughter so sad and troubled looking?"

"She has reason for being sad and troubled," said the damsel, who was called Sea Swan, "for she thinks she may have to marry a man whom she thinks little of."

"Why should that be?" said Mell.

"Because her father has promised to give her and half his Kingdom to the one who will defeat the Red Champion who has come from across the sea and who demands that the King give him tribute from the land. And the only one who has gone forth against the champion is the cook's son—a gray-faced fellow that only a kitchen maid would marry. And if it happens that the cook's son overcomes the Red Champion, then Princess Bright Brow will have to marry him."

And later on Sea Swan said to Mell, "The King's daughter is so troubled that she would go away to the Island of the Shadow of the Stars if she had the jewel that would bring her there. She had it once, but a fairy woman came out of the green rath and made Bright Brow give it to her."

When the feast was at its height the King stood up and bade the cook's son come near the high chair and tell how he had fought with the Red Champion that day.

The cook's son came up holding the red plume in his hand. He told a story of how he had fought with the Red Champion all the day and how he had beaten him back to his boat and how he had made him take his boat out to sea, and how, as the champion had sprung into the boat, he had struck at him and had cut the red plume from his cap. "And I shall go down to the seashore tomorrow," said the cook's son very bravely, "and if the Red Champion dares come back I shall take off his head instead of his plume."

Then he left the red plume beside the King's daughter and her father made Bright Brow hold up her forehead for the cook's son to kiss. And all in the supper-room clapped their hands for the cook's son.

The next day Mell, the hen-wife's son, stood outside the cookhouse and he heard a tremendous rattling within.

"That is the cook's son preparing to go out to battle," said one of the grooms. "He is striking the ladles upon the pot-lids to show how fierce he is."

Just as that was being said the cook's son walked out of the cookhouse. He looked around him very haughtily. Then he walked away with his big sword trailing behind him and his breastplate all to one side. Mell, the hen-wife's son, followed him.

When he came to the seashore he stood for a while looking out to sea with his knees knocking together. Then he went where he had gone the day before. He climbed into a cave in the face of the cliff and he drew the bush over the entrance so that it was quite hidden.

Mell, the hen-wife's son, looked out to sea and saw the boat that moved of itself come towards the shore. The Red Champion was in it. He sprang out on the strand, struck his sword on his shield and made proclamation: Unless the King of the land sent a champion who could overthrow him he would make him pay tribute for his kingdom.

Then down to meet him came Mell, the hen-wife's son, his sword in his hand. He and the Red

Champion saluted each other and then fought together. They trampled over the beach, making the soft places hard and the hard places soft with the dint of their trampling.

"A good champion, by my faith, you are," said the Red Champion to Mell when three-quarters of the day had been spent in fighting. And after that the Red Champion tried only to guard himself from the thrusts and the strokes of Mell's sword. He drew away from Mell and towards his boat and he put one foot in it.

"You have the honors of the day's fight, champion," said he.

"I shall have something beside the honors," said Mell and he struck at the Red Champion's belt. Down on the shingles fell the silver-studded belt and the Red Champion pushed off in his boat.

When the cook's son saw from his cave that the Red Champion had gone he came down to the water's edge where Mell was lying with his face and hands in the water to cool himself after the combat. The silver-studded belt was lying beside Mell. The cook's son took it up without saying a word and he went off towards the castle.

That night Mell, the hen-wife's son, sat by himself in the supper room of the King's castle. He watched and watched the face of the Princess Bright Brow. She looked more pale and troubled than on the night before. And after the harpers had played, the King called upon the cook's son to come up to the high chair and tell how he had battled with the Red Champion. He came up with the silver-studded belt in his hand and told a story of how he had beaten the Red Champion back into the sea. And when the story was told the King bade Bright Brow go over to him and kiss the cook's son on his heavy gray cheek.

The next day when he stood before the cookhouse, Mell, the hen-wife's son, heard a greater rattling than before. The cook's son struck the pot-lids with the ladles more fiercely than ever and he cried out in a high voice, "This is the last time that I shall ever stand amongst the pots and the pans, the lids and the ladles, for I go to fight the Red Champion for the last time, and after this I will sit beside the King's chair and the King's daughter, Princess Bright Brow, will sit upon my knee."

He walked though the street with his head high and marched down to the seashore, his long sword trailing behind him. But when he drew near the seashore his gait became less grand and his knees began to knock together. He looked out to the sea and when he saw the boat that moved of itself coming towards the shore he clambered into the cave and drew the bush around to cover up the entrance.

The boat that moved of itself came to the strand. The Red Champion sprang out on the shingles and he made his proclamation.

Then up to him came Mell, the hen-wife's son. "I will strive with you," said he, "as I strove with you yesterday and the day before. And how shall we fight? Shall it be with swords or by wrestling?"

"By wrestling let it be to-day," said the Red Champion.

They laid hands on each other and began to wrestle. And in their bout of wrestling they made holes in the ground and they made hillocks on the ground, and when the day was about to close Mell overthrew the Red Champion. He left him stark on the ground. Then he took the cord he had round his waist and he bound the Red Champion— hands and feet, waist and chest he bound him.

The cook's son came up to them then.

"As you took the red plume and as you took the silver-studded belt, take the champion too," said Mell.

Then the cook's son took the Red Champion, all bound as he was, and putting him across his shoulders, went staggering up the beach towards the King's castle.

Mell, the hen-wife's son, sat in the supper-room of the castle again that night. The King's daughter,

Princess Bright Brow, was there and she was as white as white rose-leaves, and tears were falling down her cheeks. And when the wine had been drunk out of the cups the King stood up and called upon the cook's son to come up to the high chair and tell all how he had overthrown and bound the Red Champion who would have put a tribute upon the kingdom. The cook's son came up to the high chair and he told them a story that was wonderful indeed.

And when the story was told the King said, "Loose the Red Champion whom you bound, and when he has knelt here and prayed to us for forgiveness the King's daughter will take your hands and will marry you."

"Look," said the damsel Sea Swan to Mell, "how the Princess Bright Brow is pulling the hairs from her head in her grief."

The Red Champion was brought in bound, and the cook's son began to try to unbind him. But not one knot could he loosen. He tried and he tried and he broke his nails trying.

"This is strange indeed," said the King, "for it used to be said that whoever bound could loosen also."

The cook's son tried again, and he tried again, and not one cord could he loosen from another.

Then the King's daughter Princess Bright Brow looked up. "How strange it would be," said she, "if it was not the cook's son who bound the Red Champion."

Then up the Hall came Mell, the hen-wife's son. He stood over the Red Champion and he pulled a cord here and he pulled a cord there and in a minute he was unbound.

All in the hall began to murmur, "Surely the one who unloosed him, bound him," said many people.

"He is the one who bound me," said the Red Champion, pointing out Mell, the hen-wife's son, "and besides, it was he who cut the red plume off my cap and who took the silver-studded belt from me."

"Speak up and deny what he says," said the King to the cook's son.

But when the cook's son tried to speak he stuttered and stammered and his knees began to knock together and his hands went shaking. And as the company looked at him there was not one there who believed he had fought the Red Champion. And when the cook's son looked round and saw there was not one there who believed in him he gathered the supper things off the table like an attendant and went out of the room.

"And now," said the King to Mell, the hen-wife's son, "since there is no doubt but it was you who conquered the champion, to you I give my daughter's hand. Take her now for your wife and take half of my kingdom with her."

Then Bright Brow lifted her face to Mell and put her hands in his.

"Mell," said she, "Mell, the hen-wife's son, I knew for long that you would come to me. Forgive me and love me," said she, "and I will love you from this night."

And so Mell, the hen-wife's son, and the King's daughter, Princess Bright Brow, came together again. He married her and came to rule over half her father's kingdom. They lived happy ever afterwards, of course. And Mell brought his mother out of the hut beside the poultry coop and he took her to live in the castle. And in the end his mother married the steward who had become a widower and she became the most respected dame in and about the King's castle. And as for the cook's son he is still in the cookhouse amongst the pots and the pans, the lids and the ladles.

·D·S·W·

THE GIANT AND THE BIRDS

THE GIANT AND THE BIRDS

THE cock scraped and the hens scraped and when the hens went away the cock scraped by himself. He called the hens back, and they all scraped deeper and deeper. Then something was shown; it was bright and round, and the cock and the three hens scraped until the whole of it was to be seen. It was a great ring of brass.

"Tell us how you knew the bright thing was there, Hero-Son of my Heart?" said the little slate-colored hen that was the cock's mother.

"Do, do," said the feather-legged hen.

"Tell us, Top-of-Wisdom," said the blue hen.

"You all know," said the cock, "that the earth rocks underneath the place where I crow in the morning."

"We know, O Unvanquishable," said the three hens.

"But the earth never rocked here," said the cock. "That's how I knew that something powerful was under the ground at this place. It was the ring of brass. Now it will be found and brought into the house. And when I stand here and crow in the morning the earth will rock as it does in every other place in the world."

"It will, it will," said the feather-legged hen.

"It must, O Top of Valor," said the blue hen.

"And will you tell us how the ring of brass came to be there, Hero-Son of my Heart?" asked the little slate-colored hen that was the cock's mother as the other hens were lying on the ground and scattering dust over their feathers.

And their lord the cock, standing on one leg with his comb hanging over one eye, said, "No cock of our breed ever told this story before. They would not frighten the hens with it. However, since you have persuaded me, I will tell you the tale. My grandfather told it to my father who told it to me."

It is the story of Big Man who came to this place and who wore the ring of brass that we uncovered today. He did not put it over his head as you might think from the size of the ring. No. He wore it on his arm. Never was a bigger man seen by anyone living. The whole countryside stood outside their houses to see him come over the hills. When he came to where the stone well lies he stooped down to take a drink and he drank the well dry.

The people came out of the house to meet him, and he spoke to them, and out of what he said to them they drew his story.

As I am to a bantam,[1] Big Man was to the other men of the country. And if they were surprised at his bigness, he was astonished at their smallness, for he came from a time when all were as big as he. A hundred and a hundred years before he had hunted with his companions, and he was then called, not Big Man, but Little Fawn.

And one day—a hundred and a hundred years ago it was—he had gone to chase a deer. The deer fled into a deep cave and he followed with his hounds and his sword, his trumpet and his missile-ball.[2] He went astray and fell asleep in the cave, and when he wakened up, his hounds were heaps of dust

1) A small chicken.

2) Missile-ball: I could find no information about this weapon. Later in the story we are told it is made of brass and thrown by hand. Perhaps it had spikes on it.

beside him. He went into the world, and he found that his companions were dead for a hundred and a hundred years and that the men of the earth had become smaller and smaller. In the cave he left his sword and his trumpet and his missile-ball.

The cock put his two feet on the ground and shook his red comb from over his left eye to over his right eye. Then said he: Everyone in the house was friendly to Little Fawn except one person—Murrish the Cookwoman. From the first day he came there were disputes between them.

"Big men have big appetites," said she to him the day he came, "and so tonight I will give you two eggs for your supper."

But when she handed him the eggs Little Fawn said, "It was not the eggs of the hedge-sparrow we were won't to eat in my time."

"Eggs of the hedge-sparrow!" said Murrish. "I have handed you the biggest eggs laid by the best hens in the country."

"In my time there were bigger eggs in the nest of the hedge-sparrow," said Little Fawn.

The next day she gave him a barley cake for his breakfast. He ate it and then sent the boy—Ardan was his name—to ask what else she was going to give him.

"Give him!" said Murrish the Cookwoman, "I have given him a whole barley cake, and that is enough for two men's breakfasts."

"Tell her," said Little Fawn, "that I often saw an ivy leaf that was as big as her barley cake."

"Tell him," said Murrish the Cookwoman, "that I am not here to listen to old men's romances."

Now when he heard that his words were taken as old men's romances Little Fawn was an angry man. He was hungry, for the food he got did no stay his appetite, but what Murrish said in doubt of his word gave him more hurt than his hunger did. For in his day and amongst his companions a lie was never told and nothing a man said ever doubted.

The next day he sent back the dish for more butter.

"Tell him," said Murrish the Cookwoman, "that I put a whole pat of butter on his dish—enough to do two men for two days."

"Tell her," said Little Fawn, "that often I saw a rowan[3] berry that was bigger than her pat of butter."

"The child just out of the cradle would not believe that story," said Murrish the Cookwoman.

She sent him a quarter of mutton[4] for his dinner. Little Fawn told Ardan to ask Murrish for more, as the dinner she gave him left him hungry still.

3) Rowan: a mountain ash; it has small red berries.
4) A quarter of a sheep.

"Did he not get a whole quarter of mutton for his dinner?" said Murrish.

"A whole quarter of mutton, did she say?" said Little Fawn. "Often I saw a quarter of a blackbird that was bigger than her quarter of mutton."

"A quarter of a blackbird bigger than my quarter of mutton!" said Murrish. "Tell him that if he never lied before, he lies now."

"Does she say that?" said Little Fawn. "Then I swear I shall never rest in the house nor be easy in my mind until I bring her an ivy leaf that is as big as her barley loaf, and a rowan berry that is as big as her pat of butter, and if I bring these," said he, "it may not be needful for me to get her the blackbird that is as big in one quarter as the quarter of mutton that she gave me for my dinner."

There and then he went from the house and Ardan the boy went with him. They went east and they went west, they went towards the north and towards the south, but no ivy leaf did they find that was as big as a barley loaf, and no rowan berry did they see that was as big as a pat of butter. Little Fawn was troubled and downcast. They came back to the house and Murrish the Cookwoman was pleased when she heard from Ardan that they found no ivy leaf and saw no rowan berry that was as big as her barley loaf or her pat of butter.

"There is only one I can do now," said Little Fawn," and that is to bring her the blackbird that is as big in one quarter as the quarter of mutton she gave me for my dinner. And that," said he to Ardan, "will take time and trouble and the meeting of danger."

"Time and trouble?" said the feather-legged hen. "Time and trouble?"

"Why did he say time and trouble, O Top-of-Wisdom?" said the blue hen.

"Hush now," said the little slate-colored hen that was the cock's mother. "Hush now, and let the Hero-Son of my Heart tell what's best in the story."

"Little Fawn was an old man, white-haired and feeble when he came to the house," said the Cock, and now he was nearly blind. His mind would not be at rest, he told Ardan, until he brought to Murrish and showed her a blackbird that was as big in one quarter as the quarter of mutton she gave him for his dinner. "But before I can take that blackbird," said he, "I must have a hound. There is a hound in the yard, but I have tried her and found she is weak and fearful. She will have puppies, and one of her puppies, maybe, will do." And he told Ardan to tell him when the puppies came to the hound that was in the yard.

Then one day Ardan came and told him that there was a litter of puppies with the hound.

"That is well," said Little Fawn, "and in a while we will see if one pup has the strength and courage enough to help us to take the blackbird."

He told Ardan what to do. He was to take the skin that had been stripped off a dead horse and nail this skin upon a door in the yard. Then he was to do a curious thing. He was to take up each puppy and fling it against the door.

Ardan did all this and Little Fawn stood by and heard the puppies yowling as they fell on the ground. They scampered away. Then he heard nothing except Ardan's laugh.

"Why are you laughing, my boy?" said Little Fawn.

"I laugh to see what the last puppy is doing," said Ardan.

"And what is he doing?" said Little Fawn.

"He has not fallen to the ground like the others. He has caught hold of the horse skin with his teeth and he is holding on to it."

"That puppy will do," said Little Fawn. "He has strength and courage. Take him and rear him away from the others, and when he comes into his full strength you and I will take him to hunt the blackbird that is as big in one quarter as the quarter of mutton Murrish the Cookwoman gave me for my dinner. We must make our word good this time, good lad."

Ardan took away the puppy (Conbeg they called him) from the others and reared him up. Little Fawn tested his strength and courage in many ways. At length he was satisfied. One day he put a leash on Conbeg and he told the boy to come with him. Little Fawn and Ardan and Conbeg the young hound went away from the house.

"Tis the best part of the story," said the little slate-colored hen that was the cock's mother.

"It is, it is,' said the feather-legged hen.

"And how well he tells it, the magnificent Top-of-Wisdom," said the blue hen.

"I tell it as my father told me and as his father told him," said the cock, changing legs.

The first place they went was into the cave where Big Man had lain for a hundred and a hundred years. They found there the heap of dust that was his two hounds, and they found too the missile-ball of brass and the trumpet and the great sword. They took the weapons and left the cave. They turned south and they went on and on till they came to the mountain that is called Slieve-na-Mon.[5] The boy and the man and the hound rested themselves for a while on the top of the mountain.

---

5) A mountain in County Tipperary, southern Ireland. See the map on page 151.

Then Little Fawn told Ardan to take the trumpet and put it to his mouth. He blew on the trumpet.

"O louder than ever I crowed," said the cock, "was the noise he made on that trumpet. The trees that were growing on the mountain top shook at the sound."

"Blow again," said Little Fawn.

And Ardan blew again and he blew louder.

"Now look into the sky," said Little Fawn, "and tell me what you see coming towards us."

Ardan looked for a long time, and at last he saw what he thought was a cloud coming toward the mountaintop. And then he saw that the cloud was a flock of birds. They came to the mountaintop and lighted on the ground—peewits, blackbirds, starlings, finches, linnets—and each was bigger than any bird Ardan had ever seen. The birds were hardly afraid of the hound, but Conbeg went amongst them and drove them away.

And then another cloud was seen coming across the sky, and this cloud was a flock of birds too, and they came to the mountaintop and lighted on the ground—linnets, finches, starlings, blackbirds, peewits—and each bird was bigger than the birds in the first flock.

"Loose the hound on them," said Little Fawn.

·D·G·W·O

Ardan unslipped Conbeg and the hound went amongst the birds. But they were not afraid and they attacked the hound, and only his strength and courage was so great they would have driven him off the mountaintop.

They rose up and flew away, and as they did so another flock of birds came towards the mountaintop. They lighted on the ground—peewits, blackbirds, starlings, finches, linnets—tremendous birds, far bigger than before! With beaks open and claws outstretched they flew at Ardan and Little Fawn. Little Fawn took his great sword in hand and he attacked them with such strength that the great birds flew off.

All flew from the mountain except one bird who went and sat on a rock. It was a blackbird and the greatest amongst them all. When Ardan told Little Fawn that this bird was left alone on a rock he told him to unloose Conbeg.

The hound dashed at the blackbird but the blackbird flew at him and attacked him with beak and claws. With a sweep of his wing he threw Conbeg on the ground. Then he rose up in the air and flew towards Ardan and Little Fawn.

"You will escape him," said Ardan, "but me he will kill surely."

"Put the missile-ball into my hand," said Little Fawn, "and guide my aim for my sight is poorly."

Ardan put the missile-ball of brass into his hand and guided his aim. Little Fawn threw the missile-ball and the blackbird fell down on the ground—but the bird was not killed.

"A frightening tale, a frightening tale," said the blue hen.

"So it is, so it is," said the feather-legged hen

"But you have done well to tell the hens the story, Hero-Son of my Heart," said the little slate-colored hen that was the cock's mother.

"More has to be told," said the cock, "and it is needful that it should be told now."

Murrish the Cookwoman was in the kitchen. In dashed Conbeg the hound, his eyes blazing with the fierceness of the chase. Murrish was so frightened that she ran to the door. And coming to the door she saw Little Fawn with a net on his shoulder. He came into the house and he put the net on the floor, and he showed Murrish what was in the net—a tremendous bird—a blackbird that was as big in one quarter as the quarter of mutton she had on the table. And when the net was laid down on the ground the blackbird flew up and he carried the middle of the roof away with him as he flew through it and tumbled beams and rafters down upon Murrish.

"My grandfather saw the blackbird flying towards the mountain that is called Slieve-na-Mon," said the cock. "And my grandfather told my father who told me."

"Tell on, tell on, Hero-Son of my Heart," said the little slate-colored hen that was the cock's mother, and the cock told on.

"You spoke the truth when you said that you saw a blackbird as big in one quarter as the quarter of mutton I gave you for your dinner," said Murrish the Cookwoman to Little Fawn. "And I believe you when you say you saw an ivy leaf as big as my barley loaf and a rowan berry as big as my pat of butter."

"I would only show you," said Little Fawn "that the men I lived amongst had truth on their lips as they had strength in their hands and courage in their hearts."

And from that day Little Fawn and Murrish the Cookwoman lived in peace and good fellowship, and Ardan and Conbeg grew up together and became famous, one and the other. They lived happy for long, but as the books say:—

The end of every ship is drowning,
The end of every kiln is burning,
The end of every feast is wasting,
The end of every laugh is sighing.

"And if they were here once," said the cock, "they are here no more."

"And if they are not, we are," said the slate-colored hen that was the cock's mother. "We're here, and the earth, I promise you, will shake under your feet tomorrow, no matter where you crow, Hero-Son of my Heart."

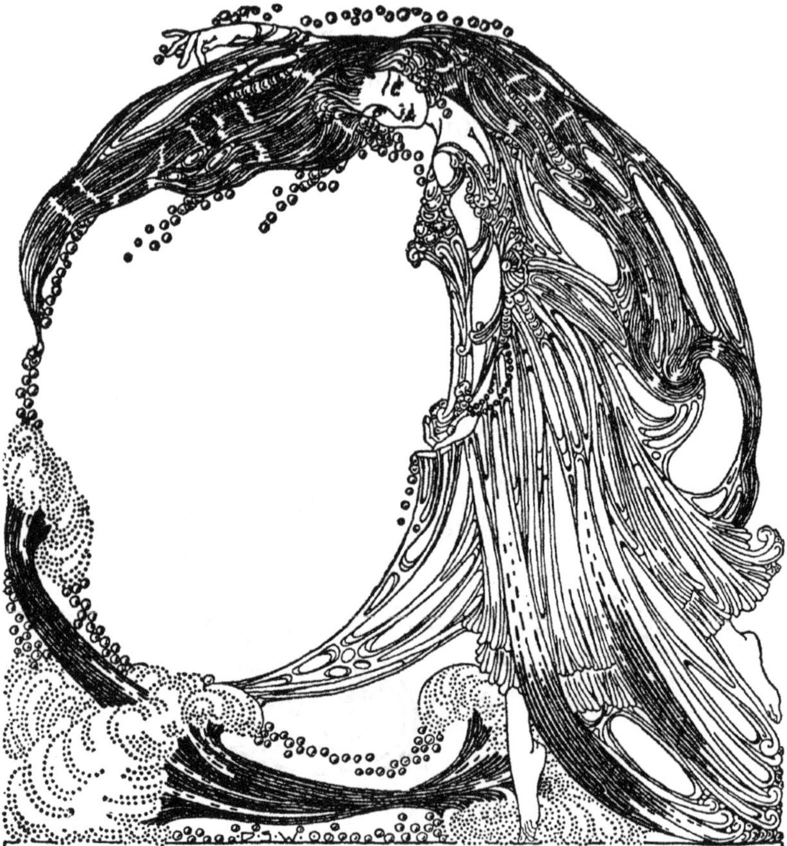

THE SEA-MAIDEN

WHO BECAME A

SEA SWAN

THE SEA-MAIDEN
WHO BECAME A
SEA SWAN

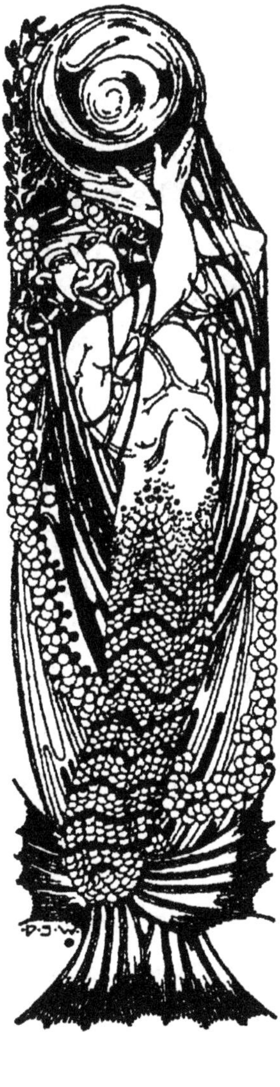

THE sea swan told the story to the pigeons of the rock, and the Boy-who-Knew-What-The-Birds-Said heard every word of it.

I was once a sea maiden, she said, and my name was Eevinn, and I was known through all the kingdoms that are underwave for my beautiful hair—my long, beautiful, green hair. Something was in me that made me want to dance, and I used to rise up through the water, and dance on the shore of the island that is called Hathony.

Mananaun, as you know, is Lord of the Sea, and what he commands in the Kingdom-Under-Wave has to be. Now Mananaun made a promise to a king of an earth kingdom, and the promise was that he would give this king whatever he asked for. The king died, according to the ways of men, and his son, whose name was Branduv, came to rule in his stead.

Branduv called Mananaun out of the sea, and he asked that he renew the promise he had made to his father. The Lord of the Sea did not want a promise to lapse because of the death of a man, and he renewed it to the man's son. Then Mananaun told him he would take him and show him the Kingdoms of the Sea and whatever he saw that he desired there would be given to him. He took him in his boat of glass, the Ocean Sweeper, to visit the Kingdoms of the Sea.

They came to Moy Mell, the Plain of Pleasure, and there Mananaun gave Branduv a branch of everlasting blossoms; they came to another kingdom and there Mananaun gave him a sword that was the best wrought in the world; they came to a third Kingdom and there Mananaun gave him a pair of hounds that could run down the silver-antlered stag. But as yet Branduv the King had asked no gift from Mananaun.

At last they came to Mananaun's own kingdom, Silver-Cloud Plain, and there Branduv was left alone while Mananaun drank the ale of the Ever-Living

Ones. Branduv saw from the shores of Silver-Cloud Plain the boat, Ocean Sweeper, and he directed that the boat bring him to the island of Hathony. And the boat travelled as the one in it wished.

Only one thing, said the sea swan, had ever made me fearful of dancing on the shore of the island of Hathony, and that was the presence of a pair of ravens. These ravens had once been sea maidens, but they had desired men for husbands, and had gone to them. But the men forsook them, and they become first witches and afterwards ravens. Ever since their change of shape they wished harm to the maidens of the sea. At first I had been frightened of them, but then I had seen them flapping about so often that I was only a little afraid.

I came up through the sea and I danced upon the shore of Hathony, and the play of the waves was in my dance, and my long soft green hair fell over my foam-white, foam-soft body. I danced on, O my listeners, and as no one had ever seen me dance, I thought no one looked upon me now.

But King Branduv of the earthly kingdom saw me. He saw me as I danced by the waves, and I was the fairest thing he had ever looked upon. At first he was all wonder and no robber's thoughts were in his mind. But the ravens came to him. One perched on one shoulder and one perched on the other, and one said, "If you carry Eevinn off you will have the fairest

wife in all the world," and the other said,"If you leave her here you will never look on anything as fair again."

The ravens flapped before him to guide him to a place in the dark rocks where he might hide and to which I would come. He followed where they led, but I saw his shadow on a rock. I drew back and the sea took me and drew me into its depth.

"The sea has taken her," said Branduv to the ravens.

"Mananaun is Lord of the Sea," said one of the ravens. "And Mananaun has promised you a gift, and he cannot refuse what you ask," said the other raven.

Then the ravens flapped away as Mananaun arrived on the island of Hathony and came to where Branduv was standing.

"You have asked me for a gift," said Mananaun. "Think now of what you desire before I take you back to your own island."

Then said Branduv, "What I ask is that you bestow upon me the sea maiden, Eevinn, who was dancing here upon the shore."

Mananaun lifted his spear in anger—but then he remembered he was bound by a promise to Branduv. He lowered the spear he had raised.

"I will give you any other gift you ask," said he, "even my own boat, the Ocean Sweeper."

"I hold you to your promise," said Branduv, "and I declare to you that I shall take no other gift unless it be the maiden who was here dancing by the sea."

"It must be then that I give her you," said Mananaun, but his face was dark.

Down he went to the Kingdom-Under-Wave and he came to the black mansion where lived the seven spinning women of the sea. He spoke as speaks a King who has a hard thing to do.

"A law has to be broken," said he.

"What law, Lord?" said the spinning women.

"The law that saves our maidens from taking part in the stormy lives of men."

"We would rather that anything else but this should happen, Lord," said the seven spinning women.

"This thing must happen," said Mananaun, "and the maiden Eevinn must go to Branduv the King."

"She must be prepared for this," said the seven spinning women.

They came to me and they told me that the man whose shadow I had seen on the rock now claimed me for his wife and that Mananaun would not gainsay him. When I heard this, O my listeners, the life nearly left me.

This comfort the seven spinning women gave me: I was to be brought to Branduv's island so that I might become used to the earthly kingdom, but my eyes were not to fall on him until the green had left my hair and the brown that the sun makes had come upon my cheeks. So I came to Branduv's island and lived by the seashore and the women of the island attended me.

How different was this earthly land from the Kingdom-Under-Wave. With us there was but the one mild season, the one mild light. Here there was glaring day and terrible darkness, bitter winds and the hot beams of the sun. With us there were songs and tales, but the songs were about love or about the beautiful things we had seen. Here the tales and songs were about battles and forays and slaying with the sword. What they told of their loves was terrible, with so much violence and unfaithfulness in them.

The soft green tints were going out of my hair and the sun was putting brownness in my cheeks. Soon my hair would be wheaten-colored like the hair of the women of the islands and my cheeks would be brown like theirs. And then the day would come when I should have to be with the man whom I looked upon as my enemy.

I used to stay by the shore and speak with the birds that came in from the sea, for I knew their language. Never again could I go back to the Kingdom-Under-Wave. Green shade after green shade left my hair, brown tint after brown tint came into my cheeks, and what could I do but envy the birds that could fly away from the islands of men. And when the green had nearly gone altogether from my hair I thought of a desperate thing to do.

I sent a message to my sisters, and I sent it by many birds, so that if my sisters did not get it by one they might get it by another. I asked in my message that they send me a draft from the Well under the Sea, and that they send it in the cup that the seven spinning women guarded. It would be terrible for any of my sisters to come to Branduv's island with the draft and the cup, but I begged that they would do it for me.

The days went by and the green color was now only a shade in my hair, and brownness was on my cheeks. The earth-women said, "Before this old moon is gone our King will come to wed you."

Then one day I found on the shore the cup I had asked for. My sisters had brought it and the draft from the Secret Well was in it. I lifted the cup in my hands and took it to where I lived.

"Come to us,' said the earth-women, "so that we may undo your hair, and see if the King may come to wed you."

They loosened my hair, and said, "There is no shade of green here at all. We will bid the King come as early as he likes tomorrow."

I lay that night with the cup beside me, and when I rose I knew I would drink from the cup my sisters had sent me—drink the draft that would change me into a bird of the sea.

And while I sat with the cup beside me and my hair spread out, Branduv, the king of the island, came to me. It may have been that I was becoming used to the sight of the people of the earthly kingdoms, for as I looked upon him he did not seem terrible to me. He looked noble and eager to befriend me and love me. But the cup was in my hands and I put it to my lips and drank it when he took a step towards me. I changed and became what I had wished to be—a sea swan.

O my listeners! Maybe it would have been well if I had wed that King and be as the women of the earthly islands. For now as I fly over the sea Branduv's look comes before me, and I remember how eager he was to befriend me and eager to love me and I am not content when flying over the sea. I am lonely here on these earthly islands, for I am now a swan, and what has a swan to do with the lives of men?

Such was the story that the sea swan told the pigeons of the rock, and the Boy-Who-Knew-What-The-Birds-Said heard it all, and never forgot a word of it.

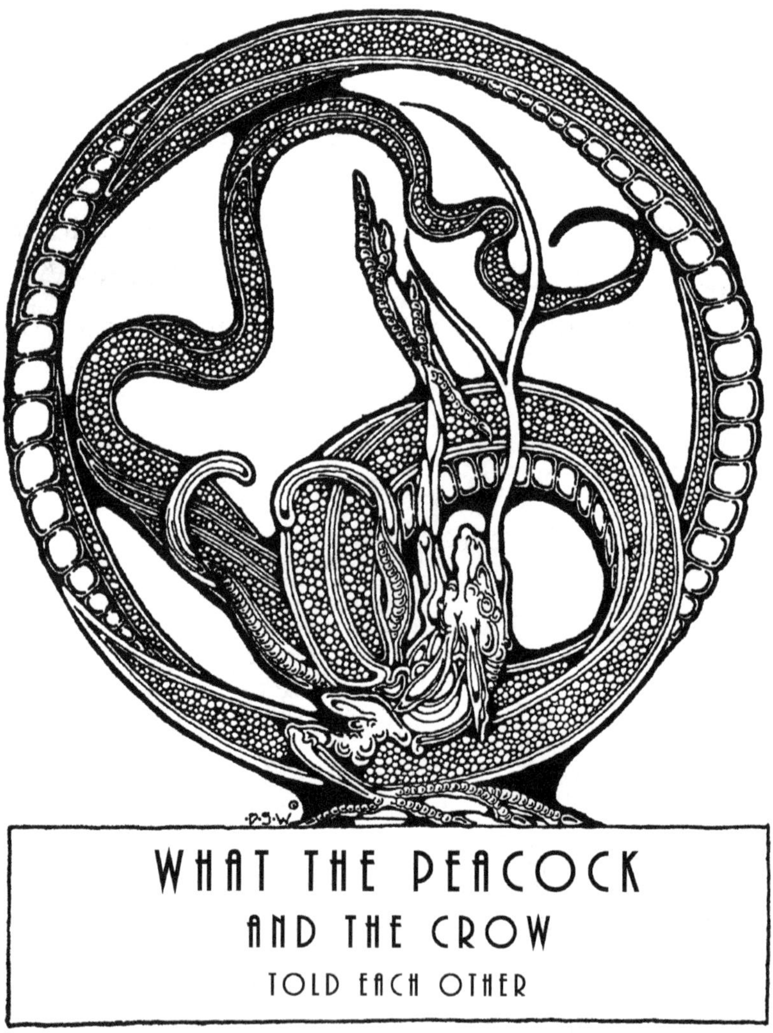

WHAT THE PEACOCK AND THE CROW TOLD EACH OTHER

WHAT THE PEACOCK AND THE CROW TOLD EACH OTHER

WHEN THE CROW CAME TO STEAL THE PEACOCK'S FEATHERS

SAID the Lapwing,
"Crow, I never have seen
Such a one as you,
Such a one as you
For stealing eggs."

Said the Crow, "Caw, caw,
I never have seen
Such a one myself,
And I am, I am sure
Longer in the world."

Then the crow flew away and the lapwing went on complaining. He flew to where the peacock was walking in the King's garden. He asked the peacock did he ever listen to stories.

"No," said the peacock as he mounted the steps of the terrace. "No. Certainly not. I do not demean myself by listening to any of the stories the commoners tell," and he turned his blue, shining neck and spread out his tail that he might view his own magnificence.

Hoodie, the grey-headed crow with the bright sharp eyes, hopped after him.

"Jewels! Kings! Magicians! Palaces! Dragons!" said the peacock. "What do geese, grouse and farmyard fowl know of such things? And yet they presume to tell stories! Stories that have nothing in them of jewels, kings, magicians, palaces or dragons!"

"There's nothing, nothing at all in them about such things," said Hoodie the Crow as he plucked a feather out of the peacock's tail.

"Yet they will not listen to me," said Purpurpurati the Peacock. "They even scorn my voice! They pretend that it is less beautiful than the cock in the farmyard and less musical than the bird's that sing at night."

"They'd say anything," said Hoodie the Crow, keeping behind the peacock's spread out tail.

Purpurpurati the Peacock mounted higher on the terrace.

"I shall walk before the statue of the beautiful queen yonder," he said, "and I shall tell you a story. The reason that I shall tell you is that the queen always listens to me. But I would have her think that it is to you that I am telling the story."

"I'll listen to you," said Hoodie the Crow and he plucked another feather out of the peacock's tail.

"When the queen has been pleased with the sight of my tail, I shall begin," said Purpurpurati, and he shook his spread out tail.

Hoodie the Crow plucked out three feathers. "How pleased she looks," said Hoodie.

"Yes, Her Majesty is always pleased by my appearance," the peacock said, and he turned round and walked the other way.

"Did I ever tell you," said Hoodie, hiding the plucked feathers behind a bush, "did I ever tell you how the pigeon went to the crow to learn the art of nest making?"

"I do not know about such things," said Purpurpurati the Peacock.

"I'll tell you then and you'll know," said Hoodie the Crow. "The crow is the master-builder among the birds and so it was to the crow that the pigeon went to learn the art of nest making.

'We begin with the sticks,' said the crow.

'I know,' said the pigeon.

'First we take one stick and lay it lengthwise.'

'I know,' said the pigeon.

'Then we put a stick across it,' said the crow.

'I know,' said the pigeon.

'And then we put another stick lower down.' said the crow.

'I know,' said the pigeon.

'Then we put another stick lengthwise.'

'I know,' said the pigeon.

'Musha,' said the crow, 'if you know so much, why do you come here at all? Away with you! Fly home now and build the nest yourself.'

The pigeon flew home, but of course he was not able to build his nest, for he knew nothing about the laying of sticks and the bringing of straws and he was too young and foolish to learn when he had the chance. And that is why the pigeon to this day cannot build a nest."

"Why do you tell such foolish stories?" said Purpurpurati the Peacock when Hoodie had finished.

"We have no other stories in our family," said Hoodie the Crow. "We don't know about jewels and magicians and palaces and kings and dragons."

"The magician," said Purpurpurati the Peacock, "lived in a palace of red marble that was surrounded by a forest of black, black trees. I lived there too and I ate golden grains out of pails of silver. That was long ago and it was far away in India.

The magician had precious stones of every kind and he would have me walk beside him to the cavern where he kept them, and as he handled them he would tell me of the virtues that each stone possessed.

One day the magician gazed upon me and said, 'This peacock I will slay, for the beauty of his neck makes dull my turquoises and the crest on his head is more shapely than my Persian jewelwork.'"

"Dear me, dear me!" said Hoodie the Crow, plucking another feather from the peacock's tail.

"Hearing him say this," said the peacock, "I flew into the branches of a dark, dark tree. And as I rested there the fair lady who walked about the garden—White-as-a-Pearl she was called and she was the magician's daughter—walked under the dark, dark trees, and I saw that she was weeping.

I knew why she wept. She wept for the young man whom her father had imprisoned in a tower. This young man was the son of a king, and the magician was his father's brother. And if the young man died the magician would become king in his brother's kingdom. But the lady White-as-a-Pearl did not want the young man to die.

·D.S.W.·

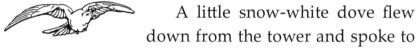

A little snow-white dove flew down from the tower and spoke to White-as-a-Pearl and asked what word she had to send to the young man.

'You must tell him terrible news, my little snow-white dove,' said White-as-a-Pearl. 'My father will have him go forth to fight a dragon. And this is a terrible dragon—every young man who has gone against him has been slain.'

The little snow-white dove flew to the young man's tower and the Princess White-as-a-Pearl stood under the dark, dark trees and wept again. And when she saw me on my branch she said, 'O most beauteous of all the birds, do you know of any arms by which a hero can slay a terrible dragon?'

I came down off my branch and I walked beside the princess, and as I walked beside her I told her the wonderful secrets I knew."

"And what were the secrets?" said Hoodie the Crow plucking the last feather from the peacock's tail. "What were the secrets anyway?"

"Can I tell secrets to a crow?" said Purpurpurati the Peacock. "Maybe not—but I have told the story so far so will tell them. I told her the secrets I had learnt from the magician when he spoke of the virtues of his precious stones—a ruby in a man's helmet would make a dragon's eyes go blind. A turquoise on his arm would make a dragon's blood turn to water. A sapphire on his spear would make a dragon's heart burst within him.

So the Princess White-as-a-Pearl went to her father's cavern and took the precious stones I spoke of and gave them to the king's son. And he went forth the next day and when he came to the dragon his eyes were blinded, his blood turned to water and his heart burst within him. Then the king's son cut off the dragon's head and brought it to the palace and the magician fled away amongst the dark, dark trees. After that I was given a red marble palace to live in."

"I lived in Lapland[1]," said Hoodie the Crow, "and who do you think I knew there?"

"No one of any great dignity," said Purpurpurati the Peacock.

"I knew your White-as-a-Pearl princess and she had become an ugly old witch-woman."

"Horrible, base crow!" screeched Purpurpurati, and he walked away up a marble stairway.

Then Hoodie the Crow dressed himself in the feathers he had stolen from the peacock and went and walked across the field admiring himself.

---

1) Lapland: a region in the artic circle in Europe. It overlaps Northern Norway, Sweden, Finland and the Kola Peninsula of Russia. The Laplanders are famous for herding reindeer. See map on page 151.

But a fox that had promised to bring a peacock to his mother-in-law saw Hoodie the Crow and stole up beside him and caught him in his mouth and carried him away. And that was the end of Hoodie who was such a clever crow.

"This peacock is very tough," said the fox's mother-in-law as she ate Hoodie.

"What would your ladyship have?" said Rory the Fox. "Peacock is always tough."

THE TREASURE OF KING LABRAID LORC

THE TREASURE OF KING LABRAID LORC

KINGFISHER-ALL-BLUE used to sit on the branch that went furthest across the stream with his head bent down and looking as if he were trying to think his head off. Only in the most lonesome places, far from where the hens cackled and the geese gabbled and the cocks crew, would the Boy-Who-Knew-What-The-Birds-Said find him. And when he did find him, Kingfisher-all-Blue would not open his beak to say one word—no, not even when the Boy would say, "Where did you get your beautiful color?" and "Why is your beak so big, little Kingfisher-all-Blue?"

Now one day when the Boy-Who-Knew-What-The-Birds-Said had left behind him the hens that cackled, the geese that gabbled and the cocks that crew, and had left behind him too the old raven that built in the lone tree, he came to where Kingfisher-all-Blue sat upon the slenderest branch that went farthest across the stream. And when Kingfisher-all-Blue saw him he lifted up his head and he fixed his eye upon him and cried out one word: "Follow." Then he went flying down the stream as if he were not a bird at all but a streak of blue fire.

Kingfisher-all-Blue went flying along the stream and the Boy was able to follow him. They went on until the stream they followed came out on the sand of the seashore. Then Kingfisher-all-Blue seated himself on a branch that was just above where the grains of sand and the blades of grass mixed with each other and he fixed his eye on a mound of sand and clay. And when the Boy-Who-Knew-What-The-Birds-Said came beside him Kingfisher-all-Blue said the one word: "Find."

Then the Boy-Who-Knew-What-The-Birds-Said began to take the sand and clay from the mound. He worked all day at it and Kingfisher-all-Blue sat on the branch above and watched him. And at evening, when all the sand and clay had been taken away, the Boy-Who-Knew-What-The-Birds-Said came upon a stone that was as big and as round as the wheel of a cart.

And when he had brushed away the grains of sand that was on the round stone he saw a writing. The writing was in Ogham,[1] but at that time even boys could read Ogham. And the Ogham writing said:

'You have luck to have seen
this side of the stone,
but you will have more luck
when you see the other side.'

When he read that he looked up to where the bird sat, but Kingfisher-all-Blue only said, "I am done with you now," and he flew back along the stream like a streak of blue fire.

The Boy-Who-Knew-What-The-Birds-Said stayed near the stone until the dark was coming on. Then he thought he would go home and in the morning speak to Pracaun the Crow and ask her about the stone that Kingfisher-all-Blue had brought him to and what good luck there was at the other side of it.

Pracaun the Crow came to the standing stone in the morning and ate the boiled potato that the Boy-Who-Knew-What-The-Birds-Said brought her, and then the Boy spoke to her about the stone that Kingfisher-all-Blue had brought him to, and he asked what good luck there was at the other side of it.

---

1) Ogham: pronounced Ah-gam, was the alphabet of the Irish in the 5th and 6th centuries. See pages 152-153 for more details and an example.

"Kingfisher-all-Blue has brought you to good luck that none of the rest of us could have shown you," said Pracaun the Crow. "Under that round stone is the treasure of King Labraid Lorc."

"Who was King Labraid Lorc and what was his treasure?" said the Boy-Who-Knew-What-The-Birds-Said.

"I will tell you first about King Labraid Lorc," said Pracaun the Crow. "He was King of this part of the country and of two lovely islands that are now sunken deep in the sea. Mananaun Mac Lir who is Lord of the Sea was his friend, and Labraid Lorc would have been a happy King only for—well, I'll tell you in a while what troubles he had.

No one knew where the King had come from. He was not born King of this part of the country nor of the lovely islands that are now deep sunken under the sea. Mananaun who is Lord of the Sea had given him the islands, or rather he had given him the two keys that had brought the islands up from the bottom of the sea. Two silver keys they were, O lad. And when they were brought together they struck each other and rang like bells and chimed out:

'Labraid Lorc is King,
King of the two Fair Islands.'

As long as he held the keys the islands would remain above the water, but if he put the keys away the islands would sink back into the sea.

Once in every month the King had a man killed. This is how it was. He would have a man shave his beard and trim his hair. This man never came alive out of the King's castle. As soon as the poor barber left the King's chamber and passed down the hall soldiers would fall upon him and kill him with their swords. Every time when the King's beard was shaved and his hair was trimmed a man was killed—twelve men in a year, a hundred and forty-four men in twelve years!

Now a warning came to a woman that her son would be called upon to be the next barber to the King. She was a widow and the young man was her only son. She was wild with grief when she thought that he would be killed by the soldiers' swords as soon as he had shaved the King's beard and trimmed the King's hair.

She went everywhere the King rode. She threw herself before him and asked for the life of her son. And at last the King promised that no harm would befall her son's life if he swore he would tell no person what he saw when he shaved the King's beard and trimmed the King's hair. After that he would be always the King's barber.

The widow's son came before the King and he swore he would tell no person what he saw when he shaved his beard and trimmed his hair. Then they went into the King's private chamber and when he came out from it the King's soldiers did not fall upon him and kill him with their swords. The widow's son went home out of the castle.

His mother cried over him with joy at seeing him back. The next day he went to work at his trade and his mother watched him and was contented in her mind. But the day after that her son only worked by fits and starts, and the day after that again he did no work at all but sat over the fire looking into the burning coals.

And after that the widow's son became sick and lay on his bed and no one could tell what was the matter with him. He became more and more ill and at last his mother thought that he had only escaped the soldiers' swords to come home and die in his house. And when she thought of that she said to herself that she would go see the druid[2] who lived at the back of the hill and beg him to come to see her son and strive to cure him.

The druid came and he looked into the eyes of the young man and he said, "He has a secret upon his mind, and if he does not tell it he will die."

---

2) Druid: a member of the ancient Celtic priesthood.

Then his mother told the druid that he had sworn not to tell any person what he saw when he shaved the King's beard and trimmed the King's hair, and that what he saw was his secret.

Said the druid, "If he wants to live he will have to speak out his secret. But it need not be to any person. Let him go to the meeting of two roads, turn with the sun and tell his secret to the first tree on his right hand. And when he feels he has told his secret your son will get the better of his sickness."

When this was told to the young man he got up off his bed and he walked to where two roads met. He turned as the sun turns and he whispered into the branches of the first tree on his right hand. And the secret that he whispered was: "King Labraid Lorc has the ears of a horse."

Then he turned from the tree and he went home. He slept, and in the morning when he woke he was well and he went to his work and he was happy and cheerful.

But the tree that he whispered his secret to was a willow, and as you know, out of the branches of the willow the harp is made. After the widow's son went away a harper seeking wood to make a new harp came by. He saw the willow and he knew that its branches were just right for the making of his harp. He cut them and he bent them and he formed a harp from them. And when the harp was finished the harper came with it to the King's castle.

The King gave a feast so that the first music that came from the harp should be honored. He made the harper sit near his own high chair. Then, when the feast was at its height, he called upon the harper to stand up and strike the first music from the new harp.

"The first music from the new harp shall be in praise of the King," said the harper when he stood up. He drew his fingers across the strings and all listened for the first music that would come. But the harp that was made out of the willow branches that the widow's son had told his secret to, murmured, "Labraid Lorc has the ears of a horse, Labraid Lorc has the ears of a horse."

The King started up from his high chair. The harper threw down the harp. Everyone was silent in the hall.

Then one voice was heard saying, "It is true. King Labraid Lorc has the ears of a horse."

The King had the man who said it taken by the soldiers and flung from the top of the castle. No one else spoke. But the next day when he rode abroad the King heard the people behind the hedges saying, "Labraid Lorc has the ears of a horse."

After that, whenever he came near them, people went from him, and at last no one was left in his castle. And there was no one to take him over to the fair islands that Mananaun, Lord of the Sea, had given him for a possession. And there was no one to bring over the fruits that grew on the islands nor the cattle and sheep that pastured there.

Then the King went to Mananaun, Lord of the Sea, and he offered him back the keys Mananaun had given him—the silver keys that struck each other when they were brought together and rang like bells and chimed out:

'Labraid Lorc is King,
is King of the two fair islands.'

But no gift that Mananaun gives is ever taken back and the keys were left with Labraid Lorc. Yet he thought he would let the keys go out of his possession so that the fair islands would sink back into the sea. But that they might not stay at the bottom of the sea forever he took the keys and he put them in a pit at the seashore and he covered the pit with a round

stone, and knowing that it would be only a lucky person who would come to that stone, he wrote in Ogham:

'You have luck to have seen this side
of the stone,
but you will have more luck when you see
the other side.'

He left the silver keys there and the fair islands began to sink in the water. So slow were they in sinking that the cattle and sheep that pastured on the islands were taken off in boats and the people who lived in villages on the islands came away with all they owned. But at last the islands sank altogether out of sight. And after they went down into the sea King Labraid Lorc was seen no more."

"And you, O Boy," said Pracaun the Crow, "are the lucky one that the King hid the silver keys for. When you take them into your hands the islands will begin to rise above the water and when they are altogether risen and are called the Fair Islands again you will be lord of them. And Kingfisher-all-Blue, the one we thought had no care but for himself, brought you to this good fortune."

Day after day the Boy-Who-Knew-What-The-Birds-Said went down to the seashore and worked to lift up the round stone that was over the pit in which King Labraid Lorc had put his silver keys. And one day he was able to raise up the stone. There lay the great keys, shining in their silver brightness. He took them up, and when he brought them near each other they struck together and rang like bells. 'Mananaun' was the name they chimed out. And they chimed again:

'Ernan is Lord, is Lord of the Fair Islands.'

Looking out to sea, the boy Ernan saw water rising up as though whales were spouting fountains, And the next day when he came to the seashore he saw that islands had risen and that they were already covered with green.

No longer did Ernan listen to what the birds said but watched the islands every day and he saw trees and grass come upon them. And when the people came and said, "Who can be Lord of these islands?" he held up the silver keys and brought them together so that they struck each other and rang like bells and chimed out:

'Ernan is Lord, Lord of the Fair Islands.'

Each day the islands grew fairer in the sight of the people, and Ernan was called, not the Boy-Who-Knew-What-The-Birds-Said, but:

Ernan, Lord of the Fair Islands

·THE·END·

PADRAIC COLUM: a brief biography

Padraic Colum was born the son of the master of a workhouse, a home for the destitute, in County Longford, Ireland, in 1881. Because of his father's work and his travels with his poultry dealer uncle around the countryside he saw the poverty and hunger of the Irish people at that time, and met many who had survived the disastrous Irish Famine of his parent's time in which about a million people died of hunger and disease and another million had to leave the country. This meant that in the space of a few years about a quarter of all the people of Ireland had either died or left. At this time he also met the wandering people of the roads who were ballad singers and storytellers—a tradition still alive at that period. These people wandered on foot from town to town and village to village and were housed and fed in exchange for their tales and poems and songs.

Ireland is a small island, only 300 miles at its longest and less than 200 miles at it's widest, and yet it has produced some of the greatest writers and poets ever: James Joyce, William Butler Yeats, Oscar Wild, George Bernard Shaw, Oliver Goldsmith, Samuel Beckett, Sean O'Casey, Patrick Kavanagh, Seamus Heaney, J. M. Singe, George Russell (AE) ... the list goes on and on—and on! Only a country steeped in the beauty and love for language can produce such greatness and this is the greatness that Padraic Colum was born into and which he took up.

As a young man Padraic (pronounced Pau-drig) was involved in all kinds of literary projects in Ireland: writing poems, plays, biographies, helping to found an Irish theatre, starting literary journals and much more.

He was in the thick of it and he met and befriended many of the people active in art and literature at that time. A generous and simple person, he was especially close to the famous writer and poet James Joyce, later meeting up with him again when Padraic lived in France for three years and eventually writing (along with his wife) a biography of him called, *Our Friend James Joyce*.

Padraic was interested in Ireland's struggle for independence from England, which was reaching a critical point when he was in his twenties and thirties. He was friends with some of the great Irish patriots and fighters, Thomas McDonagh, Roger Casement, Patrick Pearse, for instance, some of whom were also poets and writers and who were later hung or shot to death by the British army following the Irish Revolution of 1916.

Padraic married another writer, Mary Maguire, at the age of thirty-one and two years later in 1914 they set sail for America to visit for a couple of months. They ended up staying for eight years. Then, after a few years in France, they moved to New York city, both of them teaching and writing. It was in America that Padraic met with financial success as a writer, playwright and poet—not least because of his books for children and young folk. After Mary died he divided his time between Ireland and America and was often on the road teaching or traveling or lecturing.

Padraic died in Enfield, Connecticut, a small town north of the city of Hartford, in 1972, at the respectable age of 90, having lived a rich, adventurous and fruitful life and leaving a long list of books behind—he wrote 61, not counting his plays!—many of which are still read and loved today.

The Birds
of
The Boy-Who-Knew-What-The-Birds-Said

Below are the birds mentioned in the book. I have drawn pictures of most of them because it always annoyed me when a bird was mentioned in a story and I didn't know what it looked like. How was I supposed to know what it looked like without closing the book and searching somewhere else?! In this book, at least, I've solved the problem.

Many of the birds mentioned are found in both North America and Europe, but the ones in Ireland, which is where the stories take place, are sometimes different. When you live in the Irish countryside, as I have, everyone knows the birds intimately. Everyone, it seems, knows their names, where they like to nest, what their songs are, whether they like to be near people or not, and what their habits and characters are like. There, birds are part of your life. In Ireland there are also birds you never hunt, such as the swan, or kill, such as the little red-breasted robin—not that there is a law against it, but rather a feeling that certain birds belong to everybody as creatures of beauty, or are connected to our hearts and lives and therefore should be left alone.

Many of the birds in Ireland, especially the little ones, have wonderful songs, and they are so used to people being around that they will often keep singing at full tilt as you walk by the hedge or wall they are perched on. They might even look at you as if to say, "What are YOU doing in MY living room?" And, of course, as elsewhere, the birds wake you in the morning with their lovely songs, and some also, like the thrush and blackbird and crow, have a different way of singing when night is about to fall.

Birds are beautiful, wonderful, amazing creatures. They are all around us our whole lives with their colorful plumage and music and have so much to give if we only pay them a little attention.

Blackbird: blackbirds in Europe are black—surprise!—though they do have a lovely orange beak. I say this because, in America and Canada, there is a common blackbird with bright red and orange/yellow bars on their wings—these are not found in Europe. The blackbird is a mid-sized bird and is regularly seen in city and country.

Chicken: In *The Giant and the Birds* Padraic Colum writes: "The cock with his hens,"—this term can apply to any male and female birds, but in this case he clearly means chickens.

Chickens have been with us for a long time. They were probably domesticated from one or more jungle fowl about 8000 years ago in southeast Asia. The rooster likes to make a lively racket in the morning especially—as most people know from experience—crying 'cock-a-doddle-doo' in English, 'kikeriki' in German, and 'kokekokko' in Japanese.

Corncrake: The corncrake lives in meadows and is very secretive. It does not like to be seen at all and hides in grass and vegetation. Its feathers are delicate shades of brown and buff, and it's call is loud and rough, a bit like

saying, 'crake-crake ... crake-crake' in a sharp, rough voice.

Crow: crows are almost everywhere in the world. They are noisy, raucous, cheeky, and very, very intelligent. They like to hang out in groups, especially in the evening when you'll see them flying in long, loose lines back to their roosts, crying: Caw! Caw! Caw!

See Hooded Crow for a drawing.

Cuckoo: The cuckoo says 'coo-coo ... coo-coo,' which is where she got her name, but when you hear her say it, she says it SO clearly and beautifully that you never forget it. She is shy and and does not like to be seen. The cuckoo lays one egg in another bird's nest and let's them bring up her chick (now *that's* lazy).

Dove: The dove and the pigeon are the same bird. They are found all over the world, in cities and the countryside. The drawing shows a rock pigeon.

Eagle: The eagle is known by everyone. The cover of this book has a painting of an eagle.

They are a large, dramatic bird of prey with a hooked beak to tear flesh and intense, fierce eyes able to see great distances. It is the national bird of the United States of America.

Finch: There are many, many different kinds of finch. The are smallish birds, about the size of a sparrow. They are usually seed eaters and often sing loudly and beautifully. They come in many different colors and patterns. See the Goldfinch below for another example.

Goldfinch: European goldfinches have a brilliant golden yellow splash of color on their wings. They also have red on their faces. To see them on a sunny day is a treat.

Grouse: Grouse are ground birds, quite chubby and large, about the size of a chicken. They live in the northern hemisphere on moorland or mountain sides or pine forests. When you are out walking, a grouse will sometimes wait in hiding until you are almost on top of it. Then it flies up with a great, noisy "explosive" flurry of wings. This gives you a huge fright, or, as the Irish say, it puts the heart crossways in you.

Shown is the Irish Red Grouse with twin red combs on its head.

Hawk: The hawk is a bird of prey. It is smaller and more agile than the eagle and hunts small birds and animals. There are many different kinds of hawk. The one drawn is a red kite found in Ireland.

Hedge-sparrow: A hedge-sparrow lives in hedges (duh!)—but they also live in woodlands and gardens. It's plumage has various shades of brown, but it has less bold markings than the common sparrow—see sparrow drawing. It is also called the dunnock, hedge accentor or hedge warbler.

Hooded crow: This crow has a grey body and black head (and outer wings and tail) and looks like he's wearing a hood. That's why Padriac Colum called him 'Hoodie'.

Jackdaw: A jackdaw is a small crow. They really like to hang out together in big flocks. If you catch a jackdaw it caws a 'Help me!' caw and in moments there will be dozens of jackdaws over your head screaming blue murder.

In Ireland they are everywhere, in all the towns and cities and countryside. They also like to hang out around the old castles and ruins dotting the countryside. Their feathers have a colorful sheen and the backs of their necks are dark grey.

Kingfisher: The kingfisher in Ireland is a special bird. No other bird there has such bright coloring. It is orange-red on the chest and vivid, brilliant, glorious, electric turquoise blue on the rump and tail. When Padraic Colum

writes about it flying like "blue-fire" he is not exaggerating—that's just how they look on a sunny day as they flash past you. As its name suggests, it lives by streams and rivers and eats small fish by diving into the water.

Lapwing: The lapwing is also called a peewit because its call sounds like, 'pee-wit'. It is a wader (which explains its long legs) and likes to live in the lowland, flying about in large flocks.

Lark: The lark found in Europe has a most wonderful song. It rises into the air and sings and sings and sings as if its heart will burst.

The poet, P. B. Shelley, wrote a long and beautiful poem about it called, 'Ode to the Skylark'. You'd never know from its looks that the lark is such a great singer for it's not a big bird and is rather dull looking in shades of brown and buff.

Linnet: The linnet is a type of finch. It is a seed eater, as you can see from its strong, stubby bill. It comes in shades of brown, but in the summer the males but on a show and add a red patch to their chest and head.

Lint-white: 'Lint-white' is an old, mostly Scottish name for the linnet.

Peacock: The male peacock has the most gorgeous, showy, proud, look-at-me-and-be-jealous-forever tail which he raises into a great fan. They have a loud (loud!) call that can be heard for a great distance. It's not a very pretty call, more like a screech—and that is why the peacock complained that no one liked his voice in the story, '*What the Peacock and the Crow told each other*'.

The peacock cames from Asia and belongs to the pheasant family. It is the national bird of India.

Peewit: see Lapwing.

Pigeon: see Dove.

Plover: Plover are often seen at the sea shore. They nest on the ground and if you come close to their nest the mother will run just ahead of you peeping to get your attention and pretending to have a broken wing. As soon as she has led you away she flies off!

Raven: The raven is the biggest member of the crow family. They are all black and look just like crows except they give the impression of being a bit clunky and have larger, heavier beaks. They don't hang out in groups and generally like to be alone. Unlike crows which are not shy at all, ravens are usually shy of people and keep their distance. Ravens are said to live to an old age and be wise.

Woodpecker: These birds are heard hammering the bark of trees to dig out grubs and other goodies. They are strong flyers with squarish wings. There are many

different types, big and small, and they often have a red patch somewhere on their heads or chests.

The drawing is of the great spotted woodpecker.

Starling: In Ireland another name for the starling is 'stare'. The starling is now common in the United States and Canada. A few were brought to New England by a man from Britain who wanted all the birds mentioned in William Shakespeare's plays to be in North America. They exploded! Soon they were everywhere and now it is a bit of a pest sometimes.

A flock of starlings is called a murmuration. Sometimes they like to gather by the thousands and thousands and wheel and whirl and dive together. It is one of the most wonderful sights in nature because the whole group acts like a single being and people will stop what they are doing to stand and stare. These flocks are so big that they have brought down big airplanes who had the misfortune to fly through them.

They are mostly black, but with a colorful, green-purple sheen. They are specked white on the breast and have bits and pieces of white on their backs too.

Sea-swan: a name Padraic Colum gave to a swan who lived on the sea, as opposed to a lake or river.

Sparrow: In Ireland the most commonly seen sparrow is the house sparrow—so called because they like to live close to people and their houses. In the old days the house roofs were often thatched with straw and the sparrows made their nests in them. What a racket the little ones make when they are hungry!

Stone-checker: 'Stone-checker' is the Irish-Scottish name for the wheatear—a kind of flycatcher. It is buff colored with black wings and a black mask. These birds, who are only just a bit bigger than a thrush, spend their winters in Africa, below the Sahara desert, and then travel all over the northern hemisphere in summer. One bird had a tracking device put on it and it traveled 18,640 miles from Africa to the Artic and back again in one year!!!

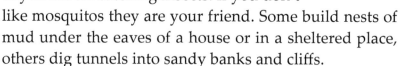

Swallow: Swallows are easy to spot because of their curved wings and divided tail (though not all of them have this.) In Ireland, and much of America too, the swallows turn up in spring when the weather gets warmer. They spend most the day in the air catching insects. If you don't like mosquitos they are your friend. Some build nests of mud under the eaves of a house or in a sheltered place, others dig tunnels into sandy banks and cliffs.

Swan: The swan is one of the world's most beautiful birds. It is large and graceful with a long, elegant neck. They are mostly white or black, or a mixture of both. They often have colorful beaks. Swans play a large part in mythology, and the story of the sea-maiden who became a swan is part of this tradition. Another famous story is *The Children of Lir* in which a stepmother changed her husband's children into swans and banned them to distant seas for 900 years.

Tom-tit: These are small birds, between the size of a wren and a sparrow. They are quick and chirpy and flit about rapidly. They have a wonderfully beady eye!

Wagtail: The Willy-Wagtail especially likes to hang out around streams catching flies. He flits from stone to stone and each time he lands he wags his tail up and down, up and down, and then takes off again. You'll see him in other places too, of course, such as your garden. They are not really shy, but they won't let you get too close either.

Wren: The wren is the smallest bird in Ireland. They are shades of brown with tiny wings, a tiny, sticking-up tail, and tiny beady bright eyes that look at you with interest. You'd think that they'd have tiny voices too— but they don't. They are quite loud and have a very complicated song. They like dense hedges and shrubs and brambles, flitting and hopping about inside them where they are safe from predators. They make neat little nests hidden away in a safe place.

Yellowhammer: The yellow-hammer is a member of the bunting family and are very similar to the finches. This bird sings, 'a little bit of bread and no cheese ... a little bit of bread and no cheese'. It has a bright yellow head and yellow chest with brownish streaks and a heavily streaked back in shades of brown. It eats seeds.

Ireland

Lapland
Artic Circle
Europe

Ulster
Connaught
Leinster
Munster
Irish Sea
Atlantic
Ocean
The Mountain of Slieve-na-Mon
mentioned in The Giant and the Birds
and where the great blackbird was fought.

OGHAM

The Ogham (pronounced Ah-gam) alphabet is thought to be named after Ogma, a strong-armed hero and warrior of myth and legend who is sometimes considered to be an Irish god. Ogham writing was used from the 4th to the 7th centuries and surviving examples are mostly found on stone markers marking a property or place. Originally the writing was most often carved onto wooden stakes, sticks or trees—the straight lines being ideal for cutting, scratching or notching wood by hand with simple tools.

All the letters in a sentence are linked together by a single line and can be written left to right horizontally (see below), or from bottom to top and left to right (see next page). There are different kinds of Ogham and the one shown here is just one example. I have given a sample word and sentence (on this page), and a long sentence around the periphery of the next page (it's a circular sentence, but it's best to imagine you are standing in the center, then, starting at the bottom left corner, read around clockwise).

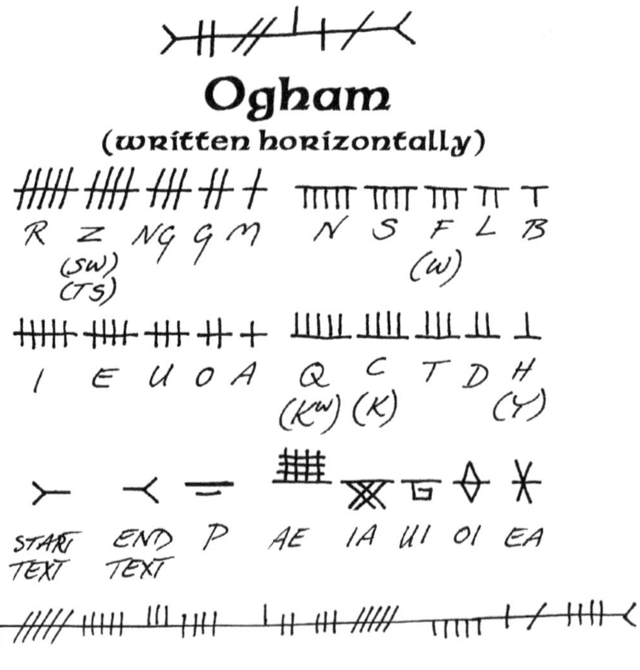

Ogham

(written vertically)

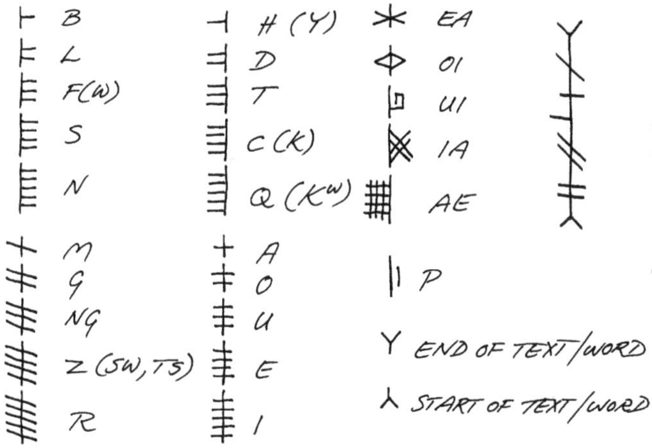

~ Selected Reviews of Books by Reg Down ~

www.tiptoes-lightly.net

The Tales of Tiptoes Lightly**:* "I wish there was something like this when my two children were growing up. It's a wonderful book." ***Book Review Cafe

The Tales of Tiptoes Lightly**:* "Our preschooler hasn't been a big chapter-book fan, but she routinely asked for another Tiptoes Story. Borrow or buy? Buy! It's a great way to introduce the chapter book concept to young readers and will be a book that middle-readers will enjoy a second (or third) time around." ***The Reading Tub Review

The Tales of Tiptoes Lightly**:* "Fabulous book! This is an amazing, wonderful, peaceful book! It's just so simple and lovely. My daughter's had these books since she was 3; she's now 7 and still loves them. I will save them for my grandchildren!" ***Amazon Review

The Festival of Stones**:* "This is a fascinating book by an extraordinarily imaginative writer." ***The Reading Tub Review

Big-stamp Two-toes the Barefoot Giant: "The adventures of Tiptoes and her friends are a constant request from my three-year-old son and seven-year-old daughter at storytime. They are timeless and are due to be classic children's stories." ***Amazon Review***

Big-stamp Two-toes the Barefoot Giant: "... my three children have fallen in love with Tiptoes Lightly! ... There is imaginative depth to this book, so we are all nourished by the repeated re-telling. ... Such a lovely childhood blessing in a world too full of cynicism, sound bites, edu-moments and videos." ***Amazon Review***

The Magic Knot: "This book is a must-have for any child, right along with all of Reg Down's books. We have read this book many times and you will not be disappointed." ***Amazon Review***

"The Lost Lagoon is a fun and recommended pick for younger readers." ***Midwest Book Review***

The Lost Lagoon: "These stories are fun and I love how they work along with the seasons and nature around us." ***Amazon Review***

The Cricket and the Shepherd Boy: "Who but Reg Down could bring us a new Christmas story that glows with such warmth and beauty? *The Cricket and the Shepherd Boy* is a gift for the Season of Love ... it will live on in the hearts of the children and adults who hear it. *The Cricket and the Shepherd Boy* is a treasure." ***Nancy Parsons, Waldorf Books***

"Also highly recommended is Reg Down's ***The Cricket and the Shepherd Boy,*** a touching holiday story that brings the generous and reverent spirit of Christmas to life year-round." ***Midwest Book Review***

The Bee Who Lost His Buzz: "Each warmhearted mini-tale blends into the next, making *The Bee Who Lost His Buzz* flow into a captivating whole. *The Bee Who Lost His Buzz* is ideal for teaching children how much fun reading can be." ***Midwest Book Review***

The Starry Bird: "Parents and children will enjoy The Starry Bird, the perfect book to send along with a favorite young person on their spring vacation or in their Easter basket." ***Midwest Book Review***

Eggs for the Hunting: ""Perfect spring tale for all ages: I fell in love with these books instantly, as did my 5 children. I think this one captures the innocence of spring and Easter beautifully. My children begged for more and I ended up reading this book in only two nights. (It) would make a wonderful gift in the Easter basket!" ***Amazon Review***

Eggs for the Hunting: "If you aren't a Tiptoes fan yet, "Eggs for the Hunting," the seventh book in the Tiptoes Tales, is a great place to start. It's a wonderful book for young children, highly imaginative and utterly entertaining." ***Waldorf Today***

The Fetching of Spring: "... an excellent pick ..." ***Midwest Book Review***

The Fetching of Spring: "... wonderful reading of the very best sort: a story true and strong, told with joy and wonder, clarity and hope. This one is not to be missed." ***Nancy Parsons, Waldorf Books***

NEW! Sir Gillygad and the Gruesome Egg

Reg Down

Sir Gillygad is a knight, a doughy knight who rides about on his trusty frog called Gorf. They venture forth on adventures bold and exciting: to the Twinkle, to Holey Hill, to the Plain of Dreams—even as far as World's End. Then rumors are heard, rumors of an egg, a Gruesome Egg, with two leggs, a left leg and a right leg, and the leggs were bird's leggs—which makes sense in an eggy sort of way. It is haunting the Daark Forest close to the Mumbly Mews and the gerwine Greneff. So off Sir Gillygad gallops (well, hoppedy-hops), there to meet and confront this unique and remarkable beast.

Sir Gillygad and the Gruesome Egg is an adventuresome tale, suitable for children aged 9 to 12 or thereabouts—and adults too, if they still are young at heart and open to the wonders that speak to the mystery of life and becoming.